LACK
OF THE
IRISH

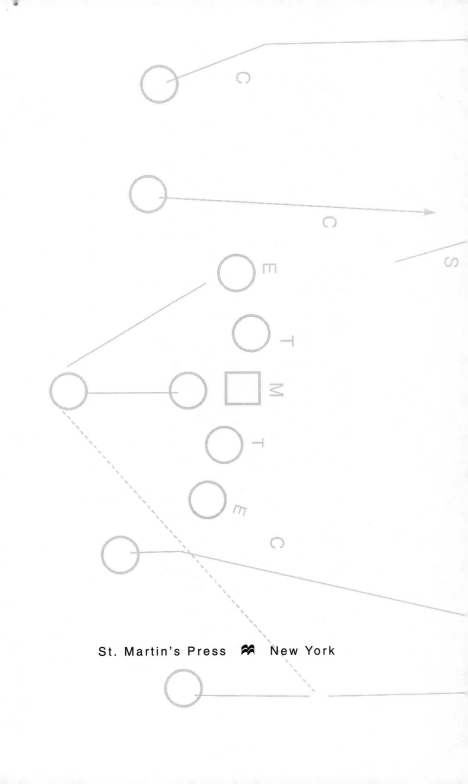

St. Martin's Press ⚏ New York

LACK OF THE IRISH

A Mystery Set at the University of Notre Dame

RALPH MCINERNY

LACK OF THE IRISH

Library of Congress Cataloging-in-Publication Data

McInerny, Ralph M.
    Lack of the Irish / Ralph McInerny.—1st ed.
        p.   cm.
    ISBN 0-312-19294-0
    I. Title.
PS3563.A31166L33   1998
813'54—dc21   98-21119
                                                            CIP

First Edition: October 1998

10   9   8   7   6   5   4   3   2   1

LACK
OF THE
IRISH

THE SCHEDULING OF A GAME
between the Notre Dame and Baylor foot-
ball teams went largely unnoticed outside the fraternity of
sportswriters and perfervid Irish football fans, but then at the
time the game lay far in the future. Past statistics are there to be
consulted like the entrails of birds, but prophecies are usually
limited to the coming season, the next game, the next play. Who
could know what the composition of the teams or indeed the
identity of the opposing coaches might be in that misty future?
But, as is the way with time, it passed, and 1998 arrived and the
great date drew ever nearer and attention began to be paid.

Student writers for *The Observer,* surveying the season's
schedule, saw the coming clash with Baylor as the moral equiva-
lent of Armageddon—that is, a notch or two above the usual game
in importance. The coaching staff predicted disaster and spoke in
awed tones of the talent on the Baylor team. Pools circulated surreptitiously under the Golden Dome and in towering Grace. Notre
Dame was favored by three touchdowns and a field goal.

In Decio, the triune office building of the faculty, professors
shuffled in slippers from office to rest room, rolling their eyes
when asked to predict the outcome of the game.

Someone observed that the Baylor game coincided with Reformation Day.

At the jock table in the University Club, incomplete sentences
were exchanged, but beneath the wariness one sensed the cock-

sure confidence that victory would be Notre Dame's. At her station inside the entrance of the dining room, from which she could easily survey her domain, Debbie the hostess and default den mother thought only of the pre- and postgame crush in the club. Parking places out front were at a premium and were assigned by lottery, leaving dozens of disgruntled losers.

"Are you going to the game, Debbie?"

"I never go to the game."

"Who's playing?"

A pause. "Ask them." And she indicated the far table, where former hockey and football coaches and their entourages sat.

A bearded, stooped man passed the hostess's station and said distinctly, "Reformation Day."

In the crypt of Sacred Heart Church, Father Green was saying Mass for several dozen members of the staff. A false ceiling now covered the pipes whose complaints and clangs once had seemed to play a liturgical role. Their sounds were muffled now. The ancient framed stations with their French legends still lined the walls, having survived redecoration. Supporting pillars marched up the center of the aisle toward the altar. Between two of them, the carpet cut to make it visible, was a pale white tombstone. The Latin legend carved into its surface was smoothed by the passage of many feet. In it lay Orestes Brownson, a man who had known the meaning of Reformation Day on both sides of the divide.

"For what else shall we pray?" the priest asked after making several requests himself. An embarrassed silence began to form until a strangled voice said, "For the success of the coming conference with Baylor and Notre Dame faculty, let us pray to the Lord."

"Lord, hear our prayer," the others said.

One or two heads turned to see who had spoken. The speaker stood with his chin on his chest. His abundant hair was wild and shot with gray. After a moment he looked up. His name was Schwartz. He was a historian. He was the organizer of the conference on which he had invoked the blessing of Almighty God.

"A conference on a football weekend?" Schwartz had been asked incredulously by an assistant provost some months before, when he had proposed an academic event to complement the athletic contest. The questioner had a narrow head, thin hair, and disproportionately wide eyes. He sensed that a request for funding was in the offing.

"On the denominational university."

Pickle, the assistant provost, waited.

"The history of the two institutions, how they differ from their secular counterparts . . ."

"You want to put Baylor and Notre Dame in the same basket?"

"I was down there for a similar conference."

"So it's already been done."

"Well, in Waco—"

"Waco?"

"That's where it is."

"What?"

"Baylor."

"But Waco's where they torched those Branch Davidians."

"That wasn't a university event."

The narrow head was being shaken. The thin lips had turned down. "I don't know."

He hadn't known for several other meetings. And then, suddenly, the atmosphere changed.

"They're Protestants, aren't they?"

"Baptists."

"Campus Ministry tells me that's Reformation Day."

"That's right."

"You need a focus."

2 THE REVEREND EDWINA MAR-
ciniak, pastor of the Independent Protestant Church of Jesus Christ and His Almighty Parent, which was located on a street in downtown South Bend that had been overlooked by urban planning and most other events of the past half century, had followed the newspaper reports of the coming clash between Baylor and the institution to the north of the city with mounting irascibility. To call the Reverend Edwina a lapsed Catholic could not capture the depth of her disenchantment with the faith of her fathers. That it was preeminently the faith of her fathers was the source of her defection and subsequent founding of the IPC as a 401c not-for-profit corporation. In the halcyon days of its foundation she had imagined women's groups across the nation rallying to her effort to supplant traditional Christianity, particularly Roman Catholicism, with a faith worthy of feminism. Little had she known of the thousands of organizations vying for the dollars of foundations favorable to the cause. Betty Friedan, Gloria Steinem, and Patricia Ireland need only lift a finger to have the media at their door providing them with free fund-raisers as they brought to the attention of viewers the outrages that women had to face daily. Sometimes Edwina suspected that the fact that she was in a church told against her.

This was puzzling. In every denomination save one, women were rising up and claiming their rightful place on the altar and in the pulpit. There was widespread dissatisfaction with the amount of progress made; laments from lady ministers and bishops were constant and undimmed by success, and Edwina had hoped to tap into that discontent. Her dream had been to drain off the women worshipers from existing churches, enlisting them in the ranks of the IPC. There had been times when she imagined herself as the veritable popess of the new dispensation, Edwina I. She began to think that her sisters in discontent wanted little more than acceptance into a fundamentally paternalistic order. Her doubts extended to her secular sisters as well. It occurred to her that her rivals were doing well in the things of this world. Such thoughts fueled her evangelistic fervor.

"We need a new reformation," she said to Kenny Keith, a retired Methodist bishop she had come upon in a local nursing home.

"Ecclesia semper reformanda," Keith squeaked. His hair was undyed but dark, his blue eyes were clear, his heart had beat within his now 110-pound frame for ninety-three years. He delighted in sharing theological discussions with Edwina.

"What does that mean?" she asked sharply.

"The church needs constant reform."

"Was that Latin?"

"Yes."

"Shame on you. I don't mean reform. I mean reformation."

Methodism had shown up somewhere late along the path of Protestantism, and Edwina wondered if it had the intensity and passion of the beginnings in Martin Luther. She had tried to talk about Martin Luther with Lutherans, but they put on little smiles and gave her to understand that much had happened since those events in the sixteenth century from which they derived their names. Her friend Fritz had told her that Catholics were more interested in Lutheran theology than Lutherans were, but he smiled when he said it, and it was difficult to know if he was telling the truth. Even if he were, it was of no help to her. She would neither sup nor talk with worshipers of the great beast and whore of Babylon.

"Nobody talks like that anymore," Fritz had protested.

"Maybe that's the problem."

That "maybe" disappeared as Edwina thought about it. The problem with Protestantism was that it had stopped protesting. Where was the original rage against the pope and all that superfluous panoply and doctrine that had distorted the faith and turned it from the simple teachings of Jesus?

"In all consistency, you should worship the Goddess and forget about Christ," Keith suggested.

"It may come to that."

But not before she had given reformed Christianity a fair shot.

Keith also found it ironic that she had settled in a city that existed in the shadow of the University of Notre Dame. But this was no accident. In her native Chicago, where her inherited faith had withered and died, Notre Dame had seemed as close as it could possibly be and still be in South Bend. The Fighting Irish took precedence over the University of Illinois and Northwestern in the Chicago sports pages, and in Catholic circles everyone was at least an honorary or subway alumnus of Notre Dame. News from the campus traveled swiftly to Chicago. Thus it was that Edwina's disenchantment with what seemed to her the paternalistic church in which she had been raised coincided with information that a group had formed at Notre Dame dedicated to the ordination of women into the priesthood. Briefly, this movement had seemed the answer to her own discontent, but Edwina was neither naive nor romantic. She had no delusion that the Catholic Church would ever ordain women. She at least had read the Roman documents that addressed this issue. She conceded them consistency and logic, granting their premises. Among her hopes when she set up church in South Bend was that her pulpit would be a magnet drawing all those alleged malcontents from the Notre Dame campus.

Alas, this was not to be. How often had she been given the old story of why a lapsed Catholic would not become a Protestant: "I have lost my faith, madam. Not my reason." Of course Edwina herself was a counterexample of this. She longed for an excuse to mount a campaign that could not be ignored.

"A *casus belli*," Kenny Keith said, looking naughty.

"The Wittenberg door!" she cried. "The ninety-five theses!"

"Were there really that many?"

It was the great event that was commemorated on Reformation Day, October 31: the nailing of those theses to the church door by Martin Luther.

And then her prayers were answered. She had read the paper almost in disbelief at her good fortune, but there could be no doubt of it. A football game had been scheduled between Baylor University and Notre Dame! And it fell on Reformation Day! This indeed was destiny. Edwina went in person to the local television stations and insisted on being interviewed. So confident was she that her cause was righteous that she was not even surprised when she made the evening news on all three network outlets.

LOCAL PASTOR TO LEAD BOYCOTT OF BAYLOR—NOTRE DAME GAME.

3 CHRISTOPHER WATTS HAD THE look of a man on the wagon who would love to tell you all about it. In the matter of liquor he had, as he put it, had his share, but the time had come when it was a choice between the pleasures of intoxication or his job, and although he drank largely to forget his job, he had made the great decision. He had not joined AA. He had not sought counseling of any kind. He had rid the house of bourbon and scotch and gin, bought a valedictory six-pack, polished it off in less than two hours, and then went to bed for a week. Quite literally, for he had applied for a week of vacation time. It was August in South Bend with weather unfit for man or beast, and he did not get out of his pajamas for a week. He rose from his bed only to have a bowl of cereal or a bowl of soup, and then it was back under the covers and oblivion. He began to believe that he could sleep the rest of his life away. After a week he rose and dressed. He had gone to bed intemperate. He got up a man who had put booze behind him for good.

Staying in bed and sleeping twenty hours a day had countered the greatest obstacle to abstinence, the thought of the future stretching soberly into infinity. It was not denying himself this glass or that that took willpower. It was shouldering the thought of all the possible drinks that one would never have, for ever and ever and ever. Or never and never and never.

This had been a week ago, and Watts considered himself a new man. He went back to his desk in the public information office at Notre Dame telling himself that he was engaged in meaningful work. His task was to compose or edit news releases telling of the endless activities taking place on campus. No respectable newspaper would carry all of these items, but it did not fall to the public information office to decide on the importance of the activities that were brought to it for public dissemination. On this particular morning he was pleasantly surprised to find that his arrival had been eagerly awaited by John Joseph Fenwick, his boss.

"What the hell is Reformation Day?"

Watts gave the question some thought. "I'll look it up."

"I could have looked it up."

"Yes. Why do you ask?"

"Some lady minister is threatening to boycott the game when we play Baylor."

"You mean she isn't coming?"

"She is going to protest it."

"So what?"

"So what! So I got a call from the office of the university attorney asking for suggestions on how to counter the threat."

"What threat?"

"I told you. She is going to lead a protest—"

"On game day? She won't get within miles of the stadium."

Fenwick fell silent. What Watts had said impressed him. After half a minute he picked up the phone and dialed the office of the university attorney.

"Cindy? Fenwick. I've been thinking about that lady minister." He stopped, and his expression indicated that he was listening. He avoided Watts's eyes. He began to nod in response to what he was hearing. "Of course, of course. Right away."

"Her suggestion is that we interview relevant faculty and get statements as to what they make of this."

Watts felt a powerful desire for liquid refreshment. Coffee was a consolation but it had its limitations. For one thing, it cleared the mind, and this was a moment when dullness and eventual oblivion exerted an overwhelming attraction. There were things he had never done sober, and interviewing relevant faculty was among them.

4   ROGER   KNIGHT   HAD   BEEN
named to the Huneker Chair in Catholic
Studies at the University of Notre Dame a year ago. He and his
brother, Philip, had moved to South Bend, both with the eager-
ness of sports fans, but Roger with the additional anticipation of
studying and teaching in the premier Catholic university in the
land. As a child prodigy at Princeton he had converted to
Catholicism, and, while he was often puzzled by some of the
things that went on in the one true Church, he had never doubted
the rightness of his decision. Not that he attributed it simply to
the reading and pondering he himself had done. Without grace
he could never have made the great leap. His youthfulness when
he received his doctorate and his weight, which ballooned to
Goodyear blimp proportions, had kept him from an academic
career; he had pursued scholarship privately. Phil was a private
detective who had eschewed Manhattan for Rye and took such
clients as came his way via an 800 number he ran in various yellow pages around the country. Roger had put him on the World
Wide Web as well, and he had become a virtual agency, his ac-
tual location a matter of indifference. The move to South Bend
presented no professional problems to Philip, so they had made
the change unhesitatingly.

It was Roger's little book on Baron Corvo, which had enjoyed
a succès d'estime, that had brought Roger to the attention of the
search committee seeking someone who could meet the specifi-
cations of the Huneker Chair. The professorship was not tied
down to any department or discipline, though a traditional aca-

11

demic careerist would not have had the scope envisaged. Roger's offbeat book and his chat with the committee member who flew to Rye to talk with him suggested that he might have been the very one the donor of the Huneker Chair had imagined. Once arrived at Notre Dame, Roger offered an occasional course, made himself generally available to students, and pursued his own research. For some months, he had been immersed in the thought of Orestes Brownson.

"Another book?" Philip asked.

"That's a good idea."

"I wasn't suggesting it."

Brownson's son H.A. had written a life of his father. Arthur Schlesinger, Jr., had developed an undergraduate thesis into a book that had retained its interest. There had been other, more industrious, less graceful efforts. But Roger wondered if anyone had yet captured the essence of the man. Often of late Roger sat in the crypt of Sacred Heart, in a pew near the tomb of Brownson, as if proximity to those mortal remains might somehow convey to him the departed spirit of the man. With closed eyes Roger would think of Orestes, unmoored from his parents as he and Philip had been, sent off to New Hampshire to be raised with Puritan strictness far from the madding crowd. The amount of formal education he had had could be counted in weeks, yet he had begun life as a teacher, which is how he had met his wife. From childhood Orestes had been driven by religion, and when he wearied of the Calvinism in which he had been raised, a tenet of which was that few were destined for salvation, he had turned to Universalism, to Brook Farm, and then to Unitarianism. It would be too much to say that he had tasted of every dish on the smorgasbord of Christianity, but his had been a stormy and changing allegiance. Preacher, journalist, controversialist, this autodidact had never felt at a disadvantage with any other mind.

Once he became a Catholic, at age forty-one, his path was

set for the thirty-two years that remained to him on this earth. European Catholics stood in awe of him. John Acton was a particular admirer, but Cardinal Newman came under Brownsonian censure. He himself was accused of heresy, but he was innocent and survived it all. Father Edward Sorin had tried to lure Brownson to Notre Dame, but the tireless battler was abashed by the teaching schedule the founder of Notre Dame proposed.

Nonetheless, he meant to come to Notre Dame eventually. He had not yet done so when he died in Detroit in 1876. He was buried in that city, but ten years later, with great pomp and ceremony, his body was exhumed and he was transported by train to South Bend. He was buried in the grave near which Roger sat thinking of the man's life. At first this basement church had been called Brownson Chapel, and a dormitory in the main building had been named after him. Today, situated behind the main building, one of the original structures still bore the name Brownson Hall.

Roger felt for Brownson the affinity one convert to the faith often feels for another. In a fuzzy ecumenical age it was refreshing to read the works of a man for whom doctrinal differences mattered. It was for such precisions that martyrdoms had been endured, blood spilled, emigration and exile suffered. It seemed fitting that so intrepid a pioneer as Father Sorin should have wanted Orestes Brownson to be a part of Notre Dame.

In my small way, Roger thought, mentally addressing the departed Orestes, I should like to fulfill the role that you did not live to fulfill.

He was almost embarrassed by the ambitiousness of the thought. Still, he grew used to it. In any case, it would be their secret, something between Orestes and himself. He did not feel he was making it public when Austin Schwartz came to him about his proposal for an academic celebration on the occasion of the Baylor–Notre Dame game.

"The provost said you were working on Orestes Brownson."

"Have you read him?"

Schwartz looked as if he wished he had learned how to lie. But he shook his head.

"Not many people seem to," Roger said.

The Brownson papers in the archives had been perused from time to time, but Whalen, an archivist, had suggested that they were all but virgin territory.

"He was always interested in clarifying Catholic doctrine for Protestants. This seemed to be largely a matter of addressing his own earlier misapprehensions," Roger observed.

Schwartz looked uneasy. "I wasn't think of a confrontational meeting."

"The game is scheduled for Reformation Day."

Roger waited for Schwartz to draw the inference. The day commemorated a confrontational event par excellence. But Schwartz threw back his head, closed his eyes, and began to speak of what he had in mind.

"In large part, it is meant to eclipse football. That game."

"Surely you're not serious."

Schwartz's eyes opened. "Do you attend football games?"

"Religiously. Don't you?" Roger asked.

"I saw a game once."

Roger had heard of the phenomenon of the faculty sports snob, the professor who professed to be unaware that games were played by university teams that attracted the attention of the nation and often beyond. Did Schwartz perhaps believe that first there had been an internationally acclaimed university and afterward someone foisted a football team on it?

"I thought the Reverend Edwina Marciniak would do the eclipsing."

"Who?"

"Surely you've heard."

The threats emanating from the IPC had not yet been covered by either *The Observer* or *The New York Times*, so Schwartz knew nothing of them. Roger briefed him on the matter, relying on the local media, and Schwartz's eyes narrowed. "You're making this up," he accused.

"Not at all."

Did Schwartz recognize here his own intention writ larger, folly upgraded to the level of farce?

"Upstaging a game may lie even beyond her powers."

Schwartz laughed dryly. "No doubt. But our seminar will take place during the week prior to the game, not seek to compete with it on the Saturday."

Clearly it would have been pointless to argue with Schwartz. Roger was determined to seize the occasion to smooth over academically the differences that divide Catholics from others.

"Have the people from Baylor agreed to this?" Roger asked.

"I have every reason to think so."

"After all, why not? They agreed to the game."

Schwartz seemed to find cogency in this analogy. "Can I count on you?"

If Roger agreed, he would have to forgo telling Philip of this project in a way that would enable his brother to appreciate the full humor of it. It would not be honorable both to make fun of Schwartz's project and to take part in it.

"You could speak on Brownson," Schwartz said reluctantly when Roger hesitated.

"In that case, I can hardly refuse."

5

AS THE CHAIR OF THE WEDNES-
day night lectures at Knights of Colum-
bus Hall on campus, Nicholas Owens was determined to put his
personal mark on the list of invited speakers. His election to this
powerful post had been due to unseasonal inclement weather
that had stranded many Knights when they were returning from
Thanksgiving vacation. He was elected by a majority of those
voting and others returned too numb and peeved to care that
they had missed the special election to replace the student who
had filled the post with distinction until it became imperative
that he take an overload of courses if he were to graduate with
his class. Sensing opportunity, Nicholas put himself forward.

When Nicholas showed Father Grosseteste, the chaplain,
his proposed list of speakers, the priest laughed.

"You're not serious."

"Of course I'm serious."

"But these professors are all . . ."

"Conservative?"

"That isn't it," Father Grosseteste said. "Balance should be
the keynote."

"There have been nothing but liberals invited to speak in
this hall since I have belonged to it, Father. Balance is precisely
what I am after."

It did not help that Nicholas had asked pointed questions
about the liturgy the chaplain conducted in the hall chapel, particularly the translations of the readings he favored. They parted
on a civil note, but from that time on it was war. Nicholas, who

wrote a weekly column for an alternative campus newspaper, *Right Cross,* did not fear censorship. Any effort to thwart his plans would become a *cause célèbre.* He proceeded to visit the professors on his list.

"Where is the Knights of Columbus Hall?" Roger Knight asked when Nicholas had tracked him down in his office in Brownson Hall. Knight was the one name on Nicholas's list that Father Grosseteste had not recognized.

"He's new, Father. I had a course from him last spring," Nicholas had explained.

"In what?"

"Recusant poetry."

"What's that?" the chaplain had wanted to know.

It had been an exciting course, with much about Campion's "Brag" and speculation that Shakespeare had intended to study for the priesthood at Douai and return to England and certain martyrdom. Knight had been full of unheard-of lore. Everything he taught linked up with Catholicism in some way, but then he held the Huneker Chair of Catholic Studies. Nicholas had begun to recite a quatrain of Campion's, but Grosseteste had waved it away.

In response to Professor Knight's question, Nicholas told him the location of the Knights of Columbus Hall and gave him a brief history of the lecture program.

"For three years we've had nothing but malcontents or flakes, theologians who resent the pope's interference in their efforts to reinterpret Christian doctrine, surly women from gender studies who spoke endlessly of rape and sexism, someone from Campus Ministry worried about homophobia."

"Hmmm."

"Come talk on something Catholic," Nicholas urged.

"That's pretty broad."

"Something you're interested in."

"What do students know of Orestes Brownson?" Roger Knight asked.

"Probably nothing. Should they?"

"Do you know who he was?"

"If I did, would I be asking you to come give a talk on him?"

Nicholas was in truth embarrassed. He often commented archly on the illiteracy of his fellow students in matters of their religion, and here was a name he had never heard of but which Knight clearly considered important.

"He's buried here at Notre Dame," Roger Knight said.

"Don't tell me any more. It will spoil your talk."

"Have I agreed?"

"What would be the best date for you?" Nicholas pressed on.

He scheduled Knight to start off the season. The talk on Brownson would be the keynote. Father Grosseteste seemed relieved. "Oh sure, Brownson."

Nicholas let it go. It bothered him that Father Grosseteste apparently knew who Brownson was and he did not. He realized that there was a Brownson Hall, an ancient building behind the main building. He looked up Brownson on UNLOC and was surprised at the number of titles in the library. One afternoon he walked up the road from the grotto to the community cemetery. It looked like a miniature Arlington, with row upon row of identical crosses. At one end were the graves of Sorin and Granger and, not far away, the grave of Father Zahm. He found the grave of Father Hudson, who had edited *Ave Maria* magazine. But Nicholas looked in vain for the grave of Orestes Brownson.

"What are you teaching this semester?" he asked Knight on another office visit.

"Nineteenth-century winners of the Laetare Medal." This medal was awarded on the appropriate Sunday in Lent every year and the recipient was always a featured speaker at the May commencement.

"Did Brownson win that?"

"It was inaugurated after his death. His son was awarded it, however."

"You said he was buried here."

"The father. Orestes. Yes, in the crypt. The basement church in Sacred Heart."

Roger hunched his shoulder. His office was in Brownson Hall, in a corridor where a dozen unimposing offices had been created for junior and adjunct faculty. Roger was the only senior, let alone chaired, professor there, but the location had a great convenience. Just outside his door was a parking lot, from which it was only a few steps to his office.

Nicholas asked if he could audit Knight's course, informally, just sit in when he could.

"Of course. Bring a friend."

Was he being facetious? In any case, Nicholas took him seriously and asked Agatha if she would like to join him.

"An extra class?" Agatha had ropes of yellow hair and the complexion to make it even more striking. The left side of her mouth was perpetually dimpled but the right side made up for it, having a skeptical cast. She was the object of Nicholas's devotion, a veritable cult of hyperdulia, as Roger Knight might have put it. Agatha, if she took cognizance of Nicholas's existence at all, did not dwell upon it.

"What do you know of Orestes Brownson?"

"Nothing," Agatha told him.

"You see? Come for a preview. Professor Knight is lecturing at Knights of Columbus Hall next Wednesday night."

"I already have a class that runs until five."

"We'll eat together. Meet me at the dining hall."

"North or south?"

Her question, with its implication of acceptance of his invitation, made Nicholas momentarily dizzy. Images of himself sweeping into the hall with the beautiful Agatha on his arm, a triumph to be put beside the triumph of persuading Roger Knight to lecture, both of these added to his surprising election, caused him to wonder if his fortunes were not in an ascending mode.

"Who is Brownson?" Agatha asked.

"I'm sworn to secrecy. Tuesday at five-ish in the south dining hall?"

She put out her hand and they shook on it.

Nicholas went to his room and wrote a dozen variations on a line of Yeats': "Only God could love you for yourself alone and not your yellow hair."

6 ↠ AGATHA HAD BEEN OVERJOYED
when Nicholas suggested that she come
to the lecture on Wednesday night. It would not have mattered
what the topic was, and her acceptance had little to do with
Nicholas himself, for his face blended into the cloud of faces that
smiled benignly on her as she went about the campus. Perhaps
they recognized her as a cheerleader. Maybe they were in classes
of hers. Romantic interest? The thought did not cross her mind
or, if it did, did so at a velocity that gave it no staying power. In
the vague and distant future a man awaited her, and a destiny
she did not want to think about until the man himself came into
view. Needless to say, that would lie years after graduation.
Agatha nursed a secret desire to be the university's next Hannah
Storm, and to go on to effervescent fame on a national network,
drawing on her enormous knowledge of sports.

This knowledge had never been the conscious object of pur-
suit. It simply happened naturally as the result of her fascination
with her brothers' activities, fueled by the fact that she herself
had no particular athletic talent other than gymnastics, which
had led her into cheerleading, as close as she could get to var-
sity sports. She would have joined the band, if it had come to
that, but she had tried out in her freshman year and made the
cheerleading squad and thus occupied a position of prominence
on the sidelines at home games and at many games played away
as well. Her brothers were all athletes. Roy played football at
Illinois, Julius soccer at St. Louis, Chet soccer at Loyola, and
George football at Northwestern. All of them had dreamed of

coming to Notre Dame, but they had gone where a scholarship was offered. Only Agatha had come to the school and the playing fields of their dreams, and she was on an academic scholarship. Without such athletic and academic talent, it is doubtful that any of the Marciniaks would have gone to college.

"Edwina is in South Bend," her mother had said, and her father growled from behind his newspaper.

"Edwina?"

"Your cousin."

"Nuttier than a fruitcake," came from behind the newspaper.

"What does she do?"

"Ask your father."

"Later" was her father's answer.

Later never came, or at least not until the week before her parents drove her to South Bend at the beginning of her freshman year.

"We could visit Edwina," her mother said, and there was a teasing tone to her voice.

Her father growled.

"My cousin?" Agatha remembered.

"Nuttier than a fruitcake."

"What does she do?"

Her father pretended to be distracted by the traffic on the Indiana Toll Road. Her mother said, "She is a lady preacher."

"How can she be?"

"She left the Church," her father roared.

"She started her own."

"Church?" Agatha asked.

"She's nuttier than—"

"Stop saying that, Ted. You haven't seen her in years."

"On purpose."

Agatha was confused. She wished now that she had sought information from another source, say, her Aunt Joanne, the family old maid who kept up on all her varied nieces and nephews.

It was a pretty good bet that she would get no clear grasp of the situation from her parents.

"Don't worry," her father said. "She won't even know you're here."

From time to time, at distant intervals, Agatha remembered that she had a cousin in South Bend. In sophomore year, down with the flu, she had flipped through the phone book, turned to the yellow pages and the entries for churches. And there it was. The Independent Protestant Church of Jesus Christ and his Almighty Parent. Pastor Edwina Marciniak. The times of services and the church's slogan—"Still protesting"—might have been printed in large type, they seemed so noticeable. Agatha closed the book and slid it under her bed. It seemed to her that if any of her roommates used that book, it would fall open to the page and reveal to the world that Agatha had a cousin who had repudiated the Church and founded a rival institution.

Religious practice among the Marciniaks might vary with time of life and whether they were away from Chicago or not, but to be a Marciniak and to be a Catholic were two ends of the same thought. An individual priest might irk an individual Marciniak from time to time, but the mark of the clan was reverence for the priesthood and bursting ethnic pride in John Paul II. A mixed marriage in the Marciniak theology meant marrying an Irish Catholic, as a cousin, Maria, had done. Her married name was Quirk, and this was an endless source of mirth and merriment for the more chauvinist Marciniaks. Agatha's father doubted whether that marriage was fully licit.

"Weren't they married by a priest?"

"A monsignor named Kelly." An impostor, in short.

Her father's ethnic prejudices had not affected his loyalty to Notre Dame. The Fighting Irish? He pointed out how many of them had been Polish.

"Or black," Agatha said.

Her father looked away.

Agatha had never looked up her cousin. For all she knew, her presence at Notre Dame was unknown to Edwina. Aunt Joanna told her otherwise.

"Of course she knows."

"How would she?"

"Because I told her."

This was plausible. Joanna sent out a quarterly family letter—"Marciniak Musings"—that tracked the doings of uncles and aunts and nieces and nephews and grandnieces and grandnephews. Only a spinster could have cultivated such family pride. Joanna was obviously thrilled with the triumphs she was able to report. The scholarships and fellowships that had been awarded to Agatha's immediate family had been duly recorded and disseminated wherever Marciniaks were to be found. Since this included Edwina, the presumption was that the South Bend pastor had read of Agatha's presence on campus.

"She might have called me," Agatha told herself in justification. "She had as much, if not more, of an obligation to contact her cousin Agatha."

Fortunately, this had not happened. With time, Agatha found herself less and less in sympathy with her cousin's attitude toward the Church. Agatha had had professors who groused about the pope and spoke in melancholy tones of a new day coming in the Church—after the pope had died. Agatha had never heard such irreverence. Some of these professors were Protestant, but they were indistinguishable from the Catholics in their impudence. She blanked it out as she would have blanked out whatever Edwina preached from her pulpit.

The call came in the spring of junior year.

"Agatha? Edwina. Your cousin. Are you free for lunch?"

"When?"

"Today."

"Where?"

"Do you have a car?"

"Yes."

"The Great Wall of China. Noon?"

"Good."

The phone went dead. There seemed to have been no moment during the exchange when she might have said she could not come. It was ten-thirty.

7 ROGER MET HIS UNDERGRAD-
uate class on Thursdays, from three until
five-thirty. It had been scheduled to meet Monday nights but that
would have interfered with football, so Roger had changed the
day. The enrollment doubled immediately, necessitating a move
from a seminar room in DeBartolo to a lecture hall. This was why
he had no hesitation in telling Nicholas that he could sit in if he
wished. Whelan from the archives was also an auditor, although
Roger referred to him as a monitor.

"When my knowledge of Orestes Brownson amounts to half
of Dr. Whelan's, the course will be over."

Whatever knowledge Whelan had of anything was likely to
remain a secret since his speech impediment kicked in whenever his audience exceeded one member, and sometimes before. With Roger Knight he had never experienced any difficulty
in speaking, but of course Roger knew better than to ask him to
speak out in the class.

A graduate student in theology was taking the course, Todd
Andrews. He had done his undergraduate work at Baylor, had
organized the Baptist students on campus, and had already
heard from his contacts in Waco of the proposed joint seminar of
Baylor and Notre Dame faculty prior to the big game.

"Professor, have you heard that Orestes Brownson has been
proposed as the focus for the conference?"

"What do they make of that at Baylor?" Knight asked.

"They're trying to find out who he is. I faxed them some materials."

Whelan had supplied these materials. Andrews himself was enthusiastic about the suggestion.

"It's important that the Catholic side not waffle," he said.

"What do you mean?" the professor asked.

Todd was a polite young man who considered himself a guest of Notre Dame as well as a student, and he would never say anything that might give offense. He managed to convey the thought that he had heard a good deal of badmouthing of Catholicism, even by Catholic professors. "If anyone at Baylor spoke that way about the Catholic Church, he would be accused of prejudice," he said.

"Who's waffling now?"

Todd clutched his chest like Sebastian taking another arrow. He agreed with C. S. Lewis that Christians got along best when each expressed undiluted what he or she believed. The search for a least common denominator to bind the Christian sects together led to blandness at best.

"Is baptism a least common denominator?" Roger asked.

A Baptist was unlikely to think of baptism as optional so far as Christianity was concerned. The difficulty was to think of it as a sacrament.

"Do that and you will soon be on the path of *Lumen Gentium.*"

Todd of course understood that the reference was to the dogmatic constitution on the Church that had come out of Vatican II. Reading it had played a major role in Roger's conversion. Admit one sacrament and the other six would soon follow and with them the priesthood, bishops, and apostolic succession.

"Are you trying to convert me?" Todd asked.

"I couldn't if I tried."

"Thanks a lot."

"Except in a secondary sense, perhaps," Roger conceded.

Todd would prove to be Roger's private liaison with the delegation from Baylor that would take part in the conference being organized by Schwartz. Schwartz had reported to Roger, with surprise in his voice, that they were enthusiastic about Orestes Brownson at Baylor.

"You know that means you have to prepare a paper," Schwartz said. "The rest of us know little about him. Someone from Baylor will prepare a comment on what you write and the discussion can take off from there."

"Surely there is someone who knows more than I do about Brownson."

"Not on this campus."

"Do you know Whelan in the archives?"

"He recommends you. Could you let me have your title soon?"

"Oh, if I am going to write a paper, I know what it will be on."

"Good."

"Brownson and the papacy."

Schwartz's smile faded. "Isn't that a little too . . ."

"It is sure to prompt a lively exchange."

"Maybe too lively," Schwartz said.

"Oh, I doubt that."

And from Waco came acceptance of the topic, perhaps not as enthusiastic as it might be, but acceptance nonetheless. Roger got word through Todd before Schwartz called to tell him.

"I am afraid they will come ready to do battle. This conference may make a mockery of the Treaty of Westphalia and start up the religious wars again."

"What topic had you thought of when the idea of the conference came to you?"

Schwartz sighed. "At one point I was going to propose 'The Denominational University: A Nussbaumian Perspective.' "

"They may find the papacy less controversial."

8 THE GREAT WALL OF CHINA WAS always crowded at noon, yet no prospective diner was ever turned away. Another table or booth always seemed to materialize to accommodate those about to go away in despair. When Agatha arrived she had to drive around in back to find a parking place, and once inside she looked into the dining area with dismay. If Edwina was in there, she could never find her. Whatever memory she had had of this wayward cousin had long since faded, and none of those waiting to be seated looked at her with recognition.

Agatha was just beginning to hope that the phone call had been the practical joke of one of her brothers when she felt a tug at her elbow. The woman who stood there was not much taller than Agatha's elbow.

"Edwina?"

"I recognized you at once."

Were there family traits to be found in this little woman with fiery eyes and a helmet of hair? Any random stranger stood a better chance of being a lost relative than this woman. But then Edwina smiled and a dozen cousins and aunts seemed to grin like skulls beneath the skin.

"Do you still practice your faith?" Edwina asked when they were still waiting in line to be shown to a table. The person ahead of them turned and looked at Edwina. Agatha felt a blush of embarrassment spread over her face. For answer, she nodded.

"That means yes?"

"Yes."

"Of course they would brainwash you out there."

"Out there" meant Notre Dame. The Great Wall was located on Highway 33, the road to Niles, Michigan, north of the toll road and thus north of Notre Dame. At the moment, all Agatha wanted was for the line to move and for them to get a table so that others would not overhear Edwina's next remark, sure to be as embarrassing as the last.

"I saw the light seventeen years ago."

"Oh?"

"I saw that it was all a pack of lies just like *that*." She snapped her fingers.

"I understand you've started your own religion," Agatha said, raising her voice. Two could play at this game. The man in front turned to take another look at Edwina. Then recognition shone on his face.

"Aren't you Pastor Marciniak?"

"I am." Edwina thrust a hand at him as if she were about to ask for his money or his life. "How do you know that?"

"I read the papers."

"You should come to my church," Edwina invited.

"Maybe I will."

"Bring a friend."

The man nodded and turned away. Agatha asked Edwina what the man had meant.

"Wait until we get a table."

"They're all Confucians," Edwina said when they had been taken to a table. Her hand swept out, indicating all the waiters and waitresses "Leave them be, I say. If God had meant them to be Christians he would have sent an apostle to China."

"He sent a lot of missionaries."

"He didn't send them. They sent themselves."

"You don't think everyone ought to be a Christian?" Agatha asked.

"I know you think they already are."

"Why would you think I think that?"

"Because you say you're a practicing Catholic. I assume that includes embracing Vatican Two. You know the beast of Rome has embraced universalism."

"Catholic means universal," Agatha observed.

"That isn't what I mean, but good try. How tall are you?"

"Five ten."

"You look athletic."

"We're all athletic in my family."

"I'm not."

"I meant my immediate family. My brothers and I."

"But not your father." Edwina laughed a loud, barking laugh. "What do you play?"

"I'm a cheerleader."

"I believe it."

"What had that man seen in the paper?"

The waiter came and they ordered, but it was not until the sweet-and-sour soup arrived, between spoonfuls and with her eyes trained on Agatha, that Edwina told her cousin of her plans for the Baylor game.

"Do you realize how many people come for a game?" Agatha asked.

"Fifty thousand?"

"Eighty thousand. You will be slightly outnumbered."

"What would you suggest?" Edwina wanted to know.

"Suggest? That you forget about it. Why would you want to do such a thing?"

"My target is Baylor even more than Notre Dame, I will be quite frank about that. Can you imagine an allegedly Protestant school having anything whatsoever to do with the bastion of Roman Catholicism?"

"Edwina, it's only a game."

"So was what they did in the Colosseum."

Edwina concentrated on her shrimp fried rice and a silence grew as Agatha nibbled on an egg roll. Despite the beginning of the conversation, she began to wonder if this unexpected get-together was not due to some residual sense of family in Edwina. Agatha had always felt unease around those for whom the niceties of religious faith were the stuff of ordinary conversation. Even some homilies struck her that way, particularly those that seemed to be a prolonged meditation on some episode in the past life of the preacher, preferably some childhood epiphany. Nicholas had assured her that young priests had been trained to preach like that. Rapport was supposedly established with the audience by recalling time recently spent renewing one's driver's license or dipping farther into the past to dwell on some event in childhood. Agatha found such sermons cloying. The short homilies given in Sacred Heart at the eleven-thirty Mass were, by contrast, to the point and edifying. Fathers Malloy and Beauchamp were masters of the short but pointed comment on the readings of the day. And how she missed Father Jenky, now an auxiliary bishop but once rector of Sacred Heart.

"How do you preach?" she asked Edwina.

The question surprised her cousin. She inhaled some rice, choked, drank off two cups of tea, and then breathed easily again. "How?"

"What method do you use?"

"You could tell me if you came to listen."

"Do you use autobiographical memories?"

"Only if they illustrate the plight of women."

Better go for neutral ground, Agatha thought. She found herself babbling about what was going on on campus, her classes, the lecture to which she had been invited by Nicholas in the Knights of Columbus Hall.

"About Brownson," she added.

"Brownson!"

"Do you know him?"

"He's been dead for more than a century. Oh yes, I know him. The man was a regular revolving door of religious affiliation. Who is the speaker?"

"One of the professors."

"I would like to hear that lecture."

"I think it's just for the Knights of Columbus."

"The boy who invited you—what was his name?"

Somewhat to Agatha's horror, Edwina jotted down Nicholas's name when she gave it.

"He lives on campus?"

"Yes."

"Do you know his number?"

"No!"

"Would it be so odd if you did?"

9　　IT ENTERS INTO THE HEART OF ANY
Catholic boy to think about the priest-
hood and wonder if perhaps God is calling him to that life. This
is particularly true of young men who come to Notre Dame. In
the male residence halls, the rector is a priest, and some of his
assistants are as well. This may be the first time the student has
known a priest well; almost unwittingly he studies the older man,
and a possible future leaps up in his imagination. The growing
identification with Notre Dame can spill over to the Congregation of the Holy Cross. After much pondering and talking it over
with several priests, a lad may decide to put his attraction to the
priesthood to the test. He may take up residence on Old College.

Old College stands on the shore of St. Mary's Lake, separated from it by the road and the lakeside footpath. It is one of
the oldest buildings on campus, made of the distinctive yellow
brick formed from the marl of the lake over which it looks. The
building has been used for a variety of purposes; over its long
history it has been restored and remodeled. In recent years it has
been the residence of students who, while not yet seminarians,
are seriously considering entering the Congregation. They have
a spiritual director, and their life is somewhat different from that
of other students. Greg Murphy, who had been Nicholas's room-
mate in freshman year, now lived in Old College, and visiting
him was for Nicholas an imaginative testing of his own attraction
to the place.

"You beat me to the punch," Greg said when Nicholas told

him of his successes with the lecture series at Knights of Columbus Hall. "We hope to get Professor Knight to come here one night. Mass, dinner, a talk."

"So ask him. I'm sure he'd want to. If he'd fit in here, that is."

"What do you mean?"

"Have you ever seen him? He's huge."

"Have you had him in class?"

"Last spring. And I'll be sitting in this fall."

Greg was taking courses that filled in gaps in his previous education, when he had not been selecting his courses with an eye to the priesthood.

"A guy named Schwartz spoke here the other night. He seemed to be less than enthusiastic about Knight."

"Oh, most of the faculty hate him."

"Hate him! Why?"

"Well, hate may be a little strong. But he is what he calls himself: an amateur. He has the degrees and all that, but this is his first academic appointment. He just knows things, all sorts of things."

"What department is he in?"

"None. They call him a university professor. He holds an endowed chair called the Huneker Chair of Catholic Studies."

"I think that was Schwartz's complaint. He thought he was too Catholic."

Roger Knight loved to dwell on the great professors who had established the academic reputation of Notre Dame and its distinctive atmosphere. John Zahm and his brother, of course, their careers beginning in the nineteenth and continuing into the twentieth centuries. The phenomenon of the bachelor don was one with which Roger felt particular affinity. Frank O'Malley was a favorite subject.

"He wrote very little, but it was always distinctive and good. He was connected with the *Review of Politics*. And of course there was Joe Evans, the first director of the Jacques Maritain Center."

Not all these heroes had been bachelors, of course. There had been Waldemar Gurian, Bob Fitzsimons, John Oesterle, Dick Sullivan. Nor was John Zahm the only priest in Roger's pantheon. Far from it. There had been two Father Wards, Leo L. and Leo R., one in English, the other in philosophy, their middle initials rendered Literary and Rational.

Once he began this roll of honor, Roger Knight went on and on. This conveyed an unusual view, that the Notre Dame of today had grown organically out of the Notre Dame of yesterday. Nicholas did not find this view shared by other members of the faculty.

"The place was a backwater."

"Most of the faculty were priests."

"They threw the master switch at ten o'clock and plunged the campus into darkness."

"No cars."

"A lousy library."

The alternative of Roger Knight's view of Notre Dame was that for all practical purposes it was now in its formative years, that the present faculty was the first respectable group in the history of the place.

"We are more and more like other universities. The best universities."

"Secularization," Roger sighed when Nicholas told him these things. "Of course the professors who told you these things enjoy national recognition."

"I don't know."

"If Notre Dame is to be exactly like other universities, why should anyone come here? They come here because it is still different. And it is different because of the men I mentioned and all those sleeping under those little crosses up the road toward St. Mary's."

"Did you go to school here?"

"Alas, no. I went to one of the places those bumptious professors would emulate. They want us to book passage on the *Titanic*."

"Can you come on Wednesday?" Nicholas asked Greg Murphy.

"What time is it?"

"Seven-thirty."

"I'll ask."

"Do you need permission?"

Greg looked at him for half a minute as if he were looking for another way to put this. "Yes."

"Tell them Orestes Brownson is the man buried in the basement of Sacred Heart."

"And you have come to praise him."

"No. Roger Knight has. Maybe that will impress them."

Nicholas himself was impressed by the fact that Greg would need permission in order to go off a hundred yards or so to hear a lecture on Tuesday night. How untrammeled by comparison his own life seemed, despite the pressure he felt of classes, papers to write, his hall duties to attend to, a million things. He could give himself permission to skip any of them if he really wanted. What would life be like if you had to account to someone else for your actions, account for your time, seek a permission that might be refused?

Nicholas stopped on the walk. A wind moved up from the lake and headed past Corby Hall toward the tunnel created by the opening between the front of the church and Sorin Hall. That tunnel could be the coldest place on campus. The leaves in the trees lining the walk moved in the breeze, making a dry, papery sound. Soon they would lose their grip and come sailing down and fill the campus with yellows and reds and browns, the colors of autumn. Once, long ago, students had pitched in to maintain the campus, but now efficient crews of mercenaries fought such battles for them. In season, platoons of tractor mowers fanned out over the campus like a tank battalion, male and female operators favoring long pigtails, which emerged from the aperture in the back of their caps and tossed and danced as they executed smart maneuvers around trees and flower beds. So too, when leaves began to fall there would be the sound of blowers and of vacuums as the leaves were gathered and suctioned and ground and bagged and trucked away.

On impulse, he turned and walked toward Sacred Heart, the wind taking him along as if on the wings of inspiration. In order to enter the crypt it was necessary to go around the church to a door at the far north end. A staircase led down to where a miniature Pietà donated by Father Hesburgh's parents, perhaps a fourth of the size of the original, came into view. Having negotiated around that, Nicholas found himself looking up the aisle in this low-ceilinged, claustrophobic place. His eye fell to the grave in the center aisle. How could he have failed to notice it before? When Professor Knight had told him this was where Orestes Brownson was buried, Nicholas was sure he was mistaken. Students did not often find themselves in the crypt, of course, but Nicholas prided himself on having a fairly good acquaintance with the campus, its many nooks and crannies and surprising treasures.

He dipped his fingers into the holy water font, blessed himself, and started up the aisle. It took an effort to make out the words engraved on the stone, and it was a minute before he realized the words were Latin. Had there been a time when the student body could be expected to understand what was written there? Nicholas stooped over and in the dim light read the legend word by word, copying them into a notebook as he did. At leisure, with the aid of a grammar and dictionary, he would translate what was written on the grave of Orestes Brownson:

HIC JACET.

ORESTES. A. BROWNSON.

QUI. VERAM. FIDEM. HUMILITER. AGNOVIT.

INTEGRAM. VIXIT. VITAM.

CALAMO. LINGUAQUE.

ECCLESIAM. AC. PATRIAM.

FORTITER. DEFENDIT.

AC. LICET. MORTI. CORPUS. OBIERIT.

MENTIS. OPERA. SUPERSUNT.

IMMORTALIA.

INGENII. MONUMENTA.

10

one-fifteen, the diners were few and far between. On this Wednesday afternoon, Otto Bird and Robert Leader, emeriti, sat at their accustomed table, rinsing down an adequate meal with a modest red wine. Not that they complained. Their palates had been numbed with martinis in the preprandial ritual that characterized their weekly lunches. New waitresses sometimes made the mistake of showing impatience with the glacial pace of the professorial lunch, but a steely glance and a word from Debbie sufficed to make the neophyte understand that this was not an ordinary table, nor were these ordinary diners.

It is in the minds and hearts of such as these two venerable gentlemen that the institutional memory of a place still lives. Others must consult histories and records and be harassed by dubious hearsay, but Professors Leader and Bird could summon the past like an old friend. Today they were responding to the account of Schwartz, who had stopped to say hello, been urged to sit, and now, twenty minutes later, was still being told what a simple matter it once had been to put on a lecture or plan a conference. Schwartz shook his head in disbelief at the simplicity that once had been.

"The buildings were open at night," said Leader.

"And the classrooms," added Bird.

And so in contrapuntal choral-like development the two men provided Schwartz with a contrast for the ordeal he was still in the midst of. He found himself countering the emeriti's tale with a numbered list of the steps he had gone through:

1. Obtain departmental agreement, something that had entailed presenting the idea to his colleagues, suffering their uninformed and often hostile questions, and then squeaking by with a single-vote majority.

2. Draw up a letter for the dean to be signed jointly by the chair and Schwartz, getting the conference on the college schedule.

3. Groveling at the provost's office for funding and in the hope that the conference would become a university and not just college event.

4. The go-ahead was made contingent on inviting Roger Knight, whose chair in Catholic studies Schwartz regarded as a para-academic appointment, but he met the enormous university professor with an eye to having a basis for telling the provost that Knight was aboard.

5. Aboard! Knight had virtually redefined the conference with his absurd suggestion that Orestes Brownson serve as the focus of the conference.

6. Schwartz had counted on his counterparts at Baylor to shoot down this idea. On the contrary. They had, after a week's delay, doubtless to discover who Brownson was, agreed enthusiastically with the suggestion.

7. The conference would now consist of a major paper by Roger Knight to be followed by a major response by Ronald Arbuthnot, the star of the Baylor faculty and the foremost Baptist theologian, noted for his self-deprecating mot that "Baptist theologian" was an oxymoron.

All this had amounted merely to a prelude, and it was not these items that Schwartz dwelled on with Bird and Leader.

Schwartz had spent the morning in the Center for Continuing Education, just south of the club, arranging for physical space for the Baylor–Notre Dame conference. Peter Lombardo had greeted him cordially, offered him coffee, told him how busy the director of the CCE was, and ticked off the number of events for which he was responsible. As Schwartz knew too well since this is what had brought him to the center, the CCE controlled the allocation of space throughout the campus for purposes other than regularly scheduled classes.

After some twenty minutes, Schwartz had been taken downstairs and turned over to Hazel Nootin, a program director. Regular jogging had done little to mold her avoirdupois into a shapely mass. Regular visits to the beauty parlor had failed to turn the natural curl of her hair to good purpose. Marriage to a jack of all trades had left her as the primary breadwinner. Her husband was much sought after by homeowners with rooms to be painted, electrical fixtures to be mounted, roofs to be repaired, bookcases and decks to be built. But Charles, affectionately known as Fig, had the annoying habit of remaining inactive after a project until the need for money arose again, at which point he would sort through the many requests for his services and regally gladden the heart of one and cast the others into the slough of despond. Hazel looked across her desk at Schwartz and saw in him the means of compensating for all the disappointments in her life.

"October?" she asked, and then with downturned mouth and a deepening frown began to shake her head as she slowly paged through her calendar.

"Only one day," Schwartz said.

She gave him a slow, grieving look. "Only one day," she repeated in wondering sepulchral tones.

"I don't expect more than fifty at the most. A fairly small room will do."

More than fifty at the most? Was that grammatical? He was afraid she would repeat that, too. Her sigh suggested that he had magnified rather than alleviated her problem. "Why don't you hang up your coat. This will take some time."

It had taken the rest of the morning. Hazel had invoked his sympathy for the difficulty of her task. He would not believe the idiotic requests that came to her. People wanting to put on a conference at a moment's notice as if they were the only ones in the university, as if Hazel and her fellows here at the CCE, swamped with work as they were, did not have to rearrange, reassign, readjust interminably to accommodate such unthinking behavior. Schwartz had the uneasy sense that she was speaking of him.

The hours passed. A room was found in the Law School, a second-floor lecture room, that was miraculously unclaimed on the date Schwartz required. Hazel sat back and wiped her brow as if she had been rolling a Sisyphean rock up a hill, only to have it roll down again, all morning. There were papers to be signed. Participants in the event would register in the CCE and be issued badges, maps of the campus, and a packet of useful information.

"There may not be thirty participants," Schwartz said, hoping there was some way this step could be eliminated. One who denied an article of faith in the ages of faith could not have shocked his co-religionists more than Schwartz shocked Hazel Nootin.

Having solemnly contracted with the CCE via Hazel, having turned over to her control the money the provost's office had allocated for the event, he watched her suddenly push back from her desk and take the signed document in both hands as if she were about to tear it in two.

"It can't be done."

"What!"

"Professor Schwartz, you have forgotten something. The date you have asked about falls shortly before a home game. I cannot provide the services of the CCE."

"But why? We've found a room, I have the money. . . ." He

stopped. Was this apparent reversal a boon in disguise? "If registering participants here is too much trouble, perhaps we could forgo that."

She looked sadly at him. "Rooms, Professor Schwartz. Accommodations. Hotels. There is absolutely nothing available that close to a home game."

"Oh, that I did think of. I will be able to put up the participants."

"Where?"

"In private homes."

The irregularity of this registered on the face of Hazel Nootin. Schwartz considered himself an intelligent man. He had taught successfully for twenty-two years. He was fluent to the point of glibness as a result. If he had ever thought of such menials as Hazel Nootin performing their nonsensical bureaucratic tasks on campus, he would have considered it the work of a minute to bring such a small mind around to his way of thinking. The morning had been a punishing experience. When at last she agreed to waive the matter of where the participants would stay while at Notre Dame, underscoring the anomalous nature of this concession, when finally Schwartz pushed his way through the doors of the center and into the clear, bracing autumn air outside, he was a broken man. Doubt had entered deep into his soul. He had been treated like an idiot and he had accepted such treatment. His victory had been won at the price of his self-respect.

All this Schwartz unburdened now on the willing shoulders of Bird and Leader, who asked him to sit and then lightly sprinkled salt in his wounds by telling him how easily such things were once managed. Still, it was consolation of a sort. These venerable men were obviously on his side. They needed no help to understand that the idiot in the morning's contest had been Hazel Nootin, not Austin Schwartz.

When he was leaving the club and had stopped to take a copy of *The Observer* off the pile near the door, he looked at the bulletin board and saw the notice of a talk at Knights of Columbus Hall. "The Body in the Crypt: The Mystery of Orestes Brownson. A talk by Roger Knight, Huneker Professor of Catholic Studies."

There was a bench there and Schwartz sat on it. Doubt and gloom returned. His fire had been stolen a second time. A student organization had beaten him to the punch. Knight would give the first fruits of his research to a gathering of indifferent students. It would doubtless be given a garbled account in the *The Observer.* Everyone would see what had happened. Schwartz's inspiration for a conference prior to the Baylor–Notre Dame game had been trivialized beyond repair. Nonetheless, he formed the resolution of slipping into the Knights of Columbus Hall and hearing that lecture.

11

Christopher Watts's desk like an accusation. The signatory of the message was, alas, well known to him: Hazel Nootin, Miss Preemptive Strike, the lady whose delight it was to convey to others that without her interference they would rightly be dismissed for incompetence. Hazel Nootin was informing Watts of something he had been in the process of writing up as an eloquent press release, a copy of which would go to the CCE and eventually filter down to the desk of Hazel Nootin. He had been in the full flight of creative composition, his fingers flying over the keyboard of his computer as on the monitor before him eloquence took on body and color and moved greenly from left to right, forming words, lines, paragraphs. He had felt at the height of his powers. And then the fax had come rattling in.

The first wave of anger passed, and he perused the message carefully, seeking mistakes, of fact or of grammar—anything that might provide a basis for a withering return of fire. But there was nothing. Rage gave way to thirst, and he found his whole system craving the counterfeit courage of alcohol.

He was still on the wagon. Or perhaps it would be more accurate to say on the wagon again. He had cheated a bit with a six-pack or two, but not a drop of liquor had passed his lips. Nor wine. Nor brandy. Only beer. Mere beer. And beer, as any serious drinker knows, is not drink.

The bitter truth was that Hazel's fax contained much that Watts had not known. Who but the CCE could first know of the precise place on campus where the conference would take place? They had had nothing to do with the inception of the idea and would contribute nothing substantial to its implementation, but because participants must register at the CCE and be issued name cards by Hazel, the conference would be numbered among her many achievements as program director. And then, as he perused the fax, a thought occurred to Watts and he picked up his phone and dialed deliberately and with an evil look.

"Hazel. Watts." He closed his eyes when she asked him to repeat his name.

"W-a-t-t-s. It is spelled the way it sounds. Unlike your own."

"What do you mean?"

"I received your fax and I have a question," Watts continued.

"What is it?"

"Your scheduling hasn't taken into account that we play Baylor the following Saturday. There will be no room in the inn or anywhere else for miles about."

There was silence on the line and Watts straightened in his chair. How would she try to cover such a mistake?

"You're right about the inn and other hotels in the area."

"Poor Schwartz."

"Why do you say that?"

"This conference meant a lot to him. I suppose you can postpone it?"

"Oh, there'll be no need for that. The sponsors have agreed to provide accommodation for the Baylor participants in their own homes."

"You're making that up!"

"No. But I am surprised that you think an organization as efficient as the CCE could possibly be guilty of so egregious—"

He hushed her by putting down his phone. What a fool he was. He had phoned in the certainty that he could humble Hazel Nootin, and she had hoisted him on his own petard. A religious man might have derived good for his soul from this reversal. Watts smacked his dry mouth and dreamed of drink.

At four-thirty he was seated on a stool in the back bar of the University Club, a double scotch and a bowl of popcorn before him and nothing on ESPN worth watching. Amanda the bartender was a matronly woman who would go off duty in half an hour to be replaced by Earl, someone for whom you could buy a drink and assess the depths to which civilization had fallen. Amanda's conversational topic of choice was her grandchildren. Watts was alone at the bar. He had often been in this position before. His drink was still untasted. Technically he was still on the wagon. It was at least logically possible that he would decide not to have that drink, that he would call for a diet Coke and devour this popcorn. Only Amanda knew he had returned to the scene of former defeats. He could get up and go out to his car and leave with no one the wiser. Why would Amanda mention it? She probably did not even know he was on the wagon. For that matter, he had told no one, lest he wallow in pride and swiftly fall. This was his secret and God's.

While these thoughts moved gently across the surface of his mind, Watts had picked up the glass and drunk from it. It was nearly empty before he realized that he was definitely off the wagon. A sense of elation coursed through him. He felt as if an enormous weight had been taken from his shoulders. He had acted without acting. Two hours later, he was asking total strangers if they knew a monster named Hazel Nootin.

"She's my wife."

"You poor sonofabitch."

The last distinct memory Watts had was of being lifted off his stool. There was a sudden sharp pain in his jaw and then darkness descended. When he came to he was looking at a squared, fireproof ceiling. He was lying on a couch. Earl was looking down at him.

"That was Fig Nootin whose wife you insulted."

"What was he doing in the club bar?"

"He's been doing some repairs downstairs. I offered him a drink when he laid off for the day."

"What did I say to offend him?"

"You called his wife a name."

"Whatever it was, she's worse." He tried to rise, but Earl pushed him back on the couch.

"Why don't you lie there until he leaves? I'll tell him you're all right."

"Tell him my lawyer will call on his lawyer."

"Come on, be serious."

"I am serious."

"I'm not going to tell him that."

Watts nodded. "Let it come as a surprise."

The ceiling squares were likely twelve-by-twelves. It would be possible to measure the room simply by counting those squares. He let his eye trail toward the wall, counting, but then he lost track of what square he was on. Still, it would be possible.

How many drinks had he had before Nootin smashed him in the face? This was all Schwartz's fault. If he hadn't had the dumb idea to hold a conference before the Baylor game, Watts would not have fallen off the wagon and been lying on a couch in the club counting the squares in the ceiling. His resentment went to Roger Knight as well. Ever since that multitalented dirigible had moored at Notre Dame he had been discovering with excitement what Watts had known for years and taken for granted. Imagine getting enthused about Orestes Brownson.

Watts had found that H. A. Brownson, Orestes's son, had been a recipient of the Laetare Medal, and was intent on working that into his press release. His press release. He thought of his computer, which he had not turned off when he left his office. On the monitor his screensaver would be showing a composite picture of former football coaches, but a touch of any key would bring up the text he had stopped working on in order to give Hazel Nootin a hard time.

Earl had said that Hazel's husband was still in the bar. Watts rolled off the couch onto his hands and knees and then got into a modified upright position. He went in a crouch to the front area of the club and into a phone booth, where he looked up Nootin and was delighted to find "Nootin, Charles & Hazel" listed. He dialed the number. A male answered.

"Mrs. Nugget?" he asked in a disguised voice.

"Just a minute."

In less than a minute the distinctive, aggravating voice sounded in his ear. "Yes?"

"Mrs. Nugget, your husband is drunk and disorderly at the University Club. Could you come pick him up?"

"Whom are you calling?"

"He said your name is Hazel."

"You said Nugget."

"Look, lady, he's breaking up the place."

"Who is this?"

"Earl." Watts beat on the wall of the booth, creating a great noise. "I got to go," he cried, and hung up.

Thus do the talented enjoy ultimate triumph over the small-minded. Watts went out to his car as exhilarated as if he had just had a double scotch. Perhaps he would stop somewhere on the way home and celebrate his victory.

12

Columbus Hall talk, Roger and his brother, Phil, had an early dinner as guests of Father Carmody at Holy Cross House. Father Carmody had been instrumental in Roger's coming to Notre Dame, as he had been instrumental in persuading a donor to give the money for a Huneker Chair in Catholic Studies.

"Roger Knight?" the provost had asked when Carmody first recommended him.

"He is one of the few men in the world who would know who Huneker is."

The provost had looked narrowly at Carmody. He would not ask who Huneker was, nor would he admit that he did not know.

"Well, that is a commendation."

With that as go-ahead, Father Carmody had approached Roger and the rest was history. Since Roger's arrival, Carmody had taken up temporary residence at Holy Cross House, the residence for aged, ill, and moribund members of the Congregation. Carmody had undergone a triple bypass and was convalescing in the building across St. Joseph Lake that he had always regarded warily. It is one thing to know that one's life must one day end and easy to agree that the Congregation is wise to have a residence on campus where its senior members can receive the care and attention they may require. In the abstract, such certainties come easily. But oh, it is a far different matter to accept that you yourself had come to the point where permanent residence at Holy Cross House might be advisable.

"What can't you do here, Father?" Roger asked. He professed to be enthralled by the thought of such an existence. So long as he had his computer, access to books, and people to talk with. "You can go to the library whenever you want, I suppose."

"We have a library here."

"I want to see it."

Wine was served with the meal, a bit of a treat that brought envious glances from other tables. Many diners had arrived in wheelchairs, and others entered slowly using walkers, canes, even crutches, and there was in their eyes a determination not to be listed among those no longer able to come to the dining hall. There had been a Mass before dinner, and a similar show of fortitude and determination, old priests getting into the chapel by one device or another and donning stoles so as to concelebrate the Mass.

"You're giving a talk on Orestes Brownson."

"That's right."

"The paper misspelled his name."

"Orestes?"

"No, Brownson. They spelled it with an *e.*"

"Would you like to come?" Roger asked the question with reluctance. The origin of this dinner invitation had been the suggestion that Phil would take Father Carmody to the lecture if he wished to hear it. Their host thought about it, and his very hesitation underscored that he no longer had the energy and mobility he had had.

"Not that it will amount to much, Father. Have you heard of the conference with the Baylor contingent before the big game?"

"What's that about?"

"Orestes Brownson."

"Good Lord. For years no one even mentioned his name and now—"

"When did people talk about him?"

Such a question sufficed to get Carmody going, and Roger and Phil settled back to enjoy the memories of a man for whom

Notre Dame was as much the center of the universe as it had been the center of his life. Alas, this was not a night like other nights. Roger was due at the Knights of Columbus Hall, and it was clear Father Carmody would not be coming with them.

"Maybe if you had given me advance notice," the old priest said.

"Next time, Father."

The next time would be the conference with the Baylor contingent.

"He forgot," Phil said when they were on their way.

"I'm almost glad he did. It wasn't a good idea asking him to come to such a talk."

Phil pulled into an area behind the residence hall and parked. "I'll help you get inside."

"What will you be doing?"

"I'll look in at the club," Phil said.

"When I'm done, I'll call you there."

"I'll stay if you want me to."

"Get out of here."

Phil had helped Roger out of the van and around to the front entrance of the hall, where a nervous Nicholas awaited him. With him was a young woman with wonderful yellow hair.

"This is Agatha Marciniak."

Roger shook her hand. He could see that the front hall of the residence was full of students. They turned out to be the overflow from the lounge. Roger could not help but feel pleased as he was guided through the crowd. He smiled at the audible comments about his bulk. There was nothing they could say that he had not already said himself.

The lounge had been rearranged for the occasion: a table set up before the fireplace, chairs and couches arranged for the audience. Here they were sitting on the floor as well as on the furniture and again there were appreciative remarks on the grotesque appearance of the speaker. Agatha was on one side of him and Nicholas on the other when they arrived at the table. Behind it was a chair of ample proportions. Roger was fitted with a lapel microphone, and when he asked whether it was on, his voice boomeranged around the lounge, to the merriment of all. Roger looked curiously at Agatha.

"You said your name is Marciniak?"

"Yes."

"There is a woman pastor in town. . . ."

"She's my cousin. She's here."

Agatha pointed and sure enough, seated in a chair near the fireplace was the unmistakable frown of Edwina Marciniak.

"You must tell me about her," Roger said to Agatha.

"She called to ask if she could come," Nicholas said. Clearly he thought Roger's asking Agatha detracted from his authority as host.

"She's my cousin."

Not an illuminating answer if one had not been following the story in the local paper. Roger now recognized other adults in the lounge. Schwartz was there, trying to look distracted, and Watts, the fellow from Public Relations. And then he realized that Nicholas was introducing him.

Almost no one speaks in public in the same way he or she ordinarily does, and Nicholas was no exception. He underwent a transformation: his voice changed, his expression was alien, and his style was the facetious one that only William Buckley can carry off successfully on his good days. Murmuring began in the lounge. Nicholas, no fool, dropped a good portion of what he had rehearsed and spoke of the speaker in a straightforward manner. One of Roger's major achievements, it emerged, was to have had Nicholas in class the previous semester. He told the audience that he personally had found Roger memorable.

"But why should you take my word? Find out for yourself. I give you Professor Roger Knight."

And he was on. He let some moments go by while silence

fell first over the lounge and then over those trying to get comfortable outside. And then he spoke as he might have to Philip, beginning with the tomb in the basement of the church, rattling off in Latin the legend engraved on it and then providing a rough translation:

" 'Here lies Orestes A. Brownson who humbly acknowledged the true faith and lived it his whole life; he stoutly defended Church and country with pen and voice and, though his body be consigned to death, the works of his mind survive, immortal monuments of genius.'

"Is this just conventional piety, or did he deserve such praise? Who was Orestes Brownson?"

He stressed of course the long relationship between Father Sorin and Brownson. He spoke of the series of articles Sorin had persuaded Brownson to write for *Ave Maria.*

"How many of you know about *Ave Maria?*"

Shrugs, blank looks, someone said, "Hail Mary."

A mistake perhaps, because Roger went on a long detour concerning the magazine Sorin had started, one of the main purposes of which was to disseminate devotion to the Mother of Jesus.

"Brownson was asked to write on Mary from the perspective of a convert from Protestantism and, in a way, he fulfilled the commission."

Brownson's odyssey from the Calvinism of his youth to Catholicism, with several stops on the way, formed the heart of the talk, and then Roger turned to the events leading to Brownson's reburial at Notre Dame.

"Clearly Father Sorin was profoundly impressed by Orestes Brownson. The more one learns about the great controversialist, the more he agrees with Father Sorin and with the words of praise engraved on Brownson's tombstone. The legacy of Orestes Brownson is a great treasure for the Church and for Notre Dame and for each of us."

Nicholas led the applause, somewhat too enthusiastically, but others joined in. A hand by the fireplace was raised and began to wave imperiously, but Nicholas claimed the right to ask the first question.

"Professor, have you any idea whether a course on Brownson was ever offered at Notre Dame prior to your arrival?"

Roger laughed. "It is only recently that courses on such heroes have to be offered so that the next generation will have some idea of who they were. When Brownson's reputation was fresh, there was no need to devote such attention to him. The great regret, I think, is that Brownson himself never gave the courses here that Father Sorin wished him to give."

The waving hand was attached to the right arm of Edwina Marciniak. Roger acknowledged her before she shook her limb loose.

"Professor," she began.

"Why don't you stand up," Nicholas suggested, not wanting to relinquish his role.

"I am standing up!"

"Would you state your name," Nicholas said, unfazed by the flare of anger in the little woman.

"I am Reverend Edwina Marciniak, founder of the Independent Protestant Church and a local pastor. My question is this: Why should a Catholic university take seriously a man who betrayed his faith? You were very skimpy on the long years when Brownson was Protestant."

"Forty-one years, to be exact. You are a Protestant, I understand."

"I can do no other," she cried, puffing out her chest and looking defiantly around.

"But you were raised a Roman Catholic."

"That was my misfortune. But eventually I saw the light."

"And abandoned the faith in which you were raised."

"It is not the same thing," Edwina said, finally seeing the point of these counter questions.

"I just wanted to establish that you have a right to be listened to despite your conversion."

"In Brownson's case it was conversions."

"Who knows what lies in the future for you?"

"I can assure you and these poor deluded students that I will never again tug my forelock to priest, bishop, or pope. God is as accessible to any of us as he is to them."

"Brownson was always sure he had arrived in port when he changed his religious affiliation," Roger commented.

"Are you saying that he might have abandoned Catholicism if he had lived longer?"

"Oh, each of us might do that, if we're not careful. Faith is a gift we can lose."

There followed a series of questions and statements. Students who were Protestants declared their love for Notre Dame; children of mixed marriages objected to Edwina's confrontational view of religious faith.

"Don't you think it matters?" Edwina asked, obviously shocked by such latitudinarianism.

"As long as a person is following his own conscience," someone said.

Roger stirred in his chair. "That is a pithy statement of the Protestant principle. I am somewhat surprised that Reverend Marciniak shies from it here because I agree fervently with her earlier insistence that it makes a great deal of difference how one professes the faith. It mattered in apostolic times. It mattered in patristic times. It mattered during the Middle Ages. It did not first begin to matter with the Protestant Reformation. I belong to the Catholic Church because it is the church founded by Jesus Christ and looked after by the Holy Spirit from its beginning to this very day."

Watts rose, steadied himself, and asked if the professor would care to relate what he had just said to *Lumen Gentium*. There were puzzled looks on some faces at this mention of the Vatican II dogmatic constitution on the Church. Roger said that it was precisely that document he had in mind when he just spoke.

"But didn't Vatican Two cast a wide net and include every-one in the Church?"

Edwina Marciniak exploded at that and said that she, for one, did not belong to the Catholic Church and there were mil-lions like her and it was the height of chutzpah to suggest that people were Christians without knowing it, let alone Roman Catholics.

Discussions and exchanges among those in the audience now rivaled any directed discussion from the speaker's table. Nicholas rose with a smile of triumphant satisfaction at the way the evening had gone and invited the audience to express their appreciation to the speaker, Professor Roger Knight.

In the crush that followed, a reporter from *The Observer* reached Roger. "Is Vatican Two Castel Gandolfo?"

"A little north of there, I think."

But she seemed to be serious. She had spent her year abroad in France and during her summer travels in Italy had stopped at the pope's summer residence. Roger told her the reference was to the second Vatican Council. Would he spell that? Nicholas stood by, his manner indicating that Roger was to show patience with the reporter. At this point Edwina arrived like a bowling ball, scattering students like pins.

"They're all brainwashed," she sputtered.

"This young lady is a reporter for the student paper," Roger said, taking Edwina's hand and shaking it vigorously. "She has been asking about the ecumenical council."

"There have been no ecumenical councils since Ephesus," Edwina said.

"What is an ecumenical council?" the reporter asked.

"Brainwash her," Roger said playfully, willing to leave Ed-wina with the reporter and let Nicholas lead him away. But Edwina grabbed his arm.

"Do you know that man?" Edwina indicated a figure who ducked out of sight when Roger Knight looked at him.

"Who is he?"

"He tells me he is editor of *The Notre Dame Magazine.*"

"Really."

"He asked me to write a defense of the ninety-five theses."

"He must be pulling your leg."

Edwina's expression indicated what her reaction to any such assault of her extremities would be. "He tells me that he published a piece by a Methodist professor in the theology department attacking the Church's teaching on Mary. In *The Notre Dame Magazine!*"

"I saw it."

Edwina's expression was that of a contestant who found that victory was not to her taste after all. Was the enemy as confused and in such disarray as this?

13 THE BODY WAS DISCOVERED BY
a campus security patrol making a rou-
tine round. There was one officer in the car, Melvin Kennedy, a
youth whose aspirations to become a United States Marine had
been dashed when he flunked the physical. He had then been
rejected by several police academies. Campus security had put
him in uniform, armed him, and given him everything but experience. He was not at first sure what he had found when he
called in.

"In the parking lot of the University Club?"

"Yeah."

"A body?"

"It looks like it. Something has been thrown over it."

"You haven't examined it?"

"I thought I should call in first."

"Good. Stay in your car. Help is on the way."

Melvin began to protest but he had been cut off.

Campus security had grown from a handful of retired po-
licemen who tended the two entrances to the university to an impressive force of uniformed men and women, equipped with
firearms and electronic communication devices, squad cars and
motor bikes and bicycles. Housed now in the former ROTC
building, their duties had expanded, along with the size of the
force. Questions had been raised in the faculty senate as to the
jurisdiction of these employees of the university and the legal-
ity of levying fines for parking violations cited by members of
campus security. Professors who had long treated disdainfully

the slips put under their windshield wipers, flinging them into their glove compartments when they did not shred them and feed them to the wind, were irate that menials should presume to treat the faculty of the university in this way.

"Why aren't they providing protection for the students, or something useful?"

"Do they have to wear uniforms?"

Whiz Perkins, assistant commandant of Campus Security, was in the main office when Kennedy's call came in, and he followed a patrol car to the scene of whatever it was. Chances were a rookie had become overexcited by a pile of leaves blown into a pattern on which his imagination could work. A body! Whiz chuckled, glad he was around for this.

Melvin was sitting sullenly at the wheel of his patrol car when the other patrol car pulled up next to his. At this hour, the parking lot of the University Club was, of course, empty. Whiz pulled up in line with the others, and three pairs of headlights lit up the grass between the parking lot and Notre Dame Avenue. It sure did look like a body.

It was a body. A woman's body. Now it seemed to Whiz providential that he was on the scene.

"Back in your cars," he ordered. "We're calling in South Bend."

There was no objection to this. Melvin and the two other officers hurried back to their cars and there was the simultaneous slamming of three doors. In his own car, Whiz put through a call to the South Bend police.

"We've got what looks to be the dead body of a woman."

Whatever control Campus Security might have had over the case evaporated at that moment. Within ten minutes, city patrol cars had arrived, and then in rapid succession an ambulance and a van from the medical examiner's office. And of course the vans from the three local outlets for the networks arrived, disgorging crews and raising their antennae toward the night sky.

An identification of the victim was made and passed in whispers through the crowd.

"Hazel Nootin."

"Apparently she worked here."

"At the club?"

"At the university."

These items were embellished and embroidered as they were transmitted so that on the morning news an account was given that suggested that the one thing the media could not for now divulge was the name of the assailant. There was no doubt that Hazel Nootin had met with a violent death.

It was while Philip and Roger were still at breakfast that the call came from the main building. Father Pickle wished to speak to Philip and wondered if he could come by the main building. Philip said that he would be there within the half hour. When he hung up, the two brothers exchanged a look. They had just been listening to the morning news.

"You know what it's about, Philip."

"I almost hope it is."

The thought that he might be of service to Notre Dame in his capacity of private investigator appealed to Philip. When Roger had been offered an appointment to Notre Dame and hesitated on the grounds of unworthiness, Philip had urged his brother to accept. Roger's reluctance had evaporated when Philip made it clear that he would make the move to South Bend with him. Roger regarded this as a sacrifice, but of course Phil's mind was full of the athletic contests he could enjoy if Roger joined the faculty. And so it had turned out. Moreover, Phil had come to know members of the coaching staffs as the result of attending so many practices. In some ways, he was more integrated into the Notre Dame community than Roger himself.

That morning, when the name Hazel Nootin was mentioned,

Roger got out the university telephone directory and discovered that the deceased had been employed in the Center for Continuing Education.

"I didn't know they did that sort of thing," Phil said. "Continuing education."

"It's a convention center, Phil. It's not what you think."

"That's an odd thing to call it." Phil's disappointment was due to the fleeting thought that he might look into taking a course.

The telephone rang again and again it was for Phil. It was Waring from the South Bend police.

"I suppose you've heard."

"The dead woman? Just heard."

"I'm on my way to campus now. Where can we get together?"

"It can't be right away."

"I'm told the university has hired you to look after their interests."

"I have a meeting shortly. I don't know how long it might take."

On the line Waring was humming. "Is your brother Roger there?"

"Yes. Just a moment."

"No, I'm nearly there. I'll drop by. He may be of some help."

Phil relayed this to Roger and wondered what Waring had meant.

"It can't be about Hazel Nootin, Phil. I know nothing about her."

Even so, Phil was not eager to leave Roger to the mercies of Waring. Was it possible that Roger could tell Waring something relevant to the murder? In any case, Phil had to go.

The university attorney, Cindy Dwyer, and Father Mayday, an associate provost, were concerned about the relish with which the local media had presented the grisly details of the death of Hazel Nootin. Phil pointed out that he only knew what he had heard on television and he could not recall many grisly details.

"When they have them, they will use them," the associate provost said. He was a wiry man with wiry hair, wary with worry and anxious to have a target for his anxieties. The university attorney, in pin-striped suit and florid tie, gave Phil such details as she had. Phil decided that he would wait until he had spoken with Waring to get a more clinically informative account.

"Why have you called me?" Phil wanted to know.

"You are a private investigator?"

"I am."

"We should like to hire you to solve this mystery as quickly as possible so that it can get off the front pages. It is ruinous to our development drive to have the campus seen as a place that is unsafe for females. Nothing could be farther from the truth. There are close to zero episodes of the kind that plague other campuses. We take exceptional precautions to make sure that it will remain the safest campus in the nation."

"You're certain there's a mystery to be solved?"

"Perhaps I express myself unfortunately. Until the explanation of the death of this unfortunate woman is had, it will tempt people to speculation, particularly the press. Your job would be to hasten the day when there are no more questions to ask and the poor woman can rest in peace."

"God rest her soul," the associate provost said, seeming to surprise himself with this belated recognition that a human being had died and, as he and Roger and on most days Phil himself believed, had immediately appeared before the throne of God for judgment as to its eternal condition. Doubtless it was understandable that in these unusual circumstances Father Mayday thought first as an officer of the university and then as a priest.

Philip settled the practical details of his employment, shook the attorney's and then the associate provost's hand, and was happy to get away from officialdom of that kind. Parents who had sons or daughters at Notre Dame deserved to be reassured about the campus on which their offspring lived. To read that the body of a woman had been discovered on campus would doubtless unsettle them.

"We have already heard from dozens," Mayday had said. His tone suggested that there would be hundreds more such calls in the course of the day.

Philip was wise enough not to make any promise that the matter would be cleared up promptly. But he vowed to himself that anything he could do to solve the mystery—he found no difficulty with the phrase in the privacy of his own mind—he would do as quickly as possible.

Even death by natural causes is a spectacle that few can consider with equanimity, particularly when the deceased has been ravaged by some dreadful disease, but when death has been caused by violence it takes a strong stomach indeed to face it in all its details. Years of detective work had done something toward making Philip less sensitive than, say, Roger and the ordinary citizen, but his accustoming to the horrible was as nothing next to Waring's. When he found that Waring had not returned to his office, he went down the hallway to speak with Emma Gulyas, the medical examiner. The autopsy on the body of Hazel Nootin was just beginning, and Phil was shown a seat in the audience of the little theater. Emma's matter-of-fact description as she examined the body, making incisions, drawing out fluids, on one occasion setting off the whirr of a saw, was a test for strong men. As often as not, Phil got such details by reading a report, which created a distance between him and the stark fact of death and the activities of the medical examiner that were necessary to bring these facts to light.

Hazel Nootin had been struck on the back of the head with an object that had cracked her skull, the blow probably bringing on unconsciousness. She then had been strangled with her own scarf, the lesions suggesting that the strangler had been behind her. Presuming that the one who struck her and the one who strangled her were the same person, it appeared that he had crept up behind her.

"Was she being stalked?"

"Not my field," Emma said.

When Phil emerged from the medical examiner's theater he thought he would never be able to eat again. Emma's examination had turned up equivocal signs that the victim had been sexually assaulted, and she was inclined to leave it at that.

"It sounds like maybe, Doctor," a reporter said.

"It's less than that."

"How much less?"

"Not impossible."

The reporter thought about it, then went on writing. He could make do with the phrase she'd given him.

Waring was not in his office, but he had returned from the scene of the crime. Phil found him in the cafeteria. Before he remembered, he had settled down with coffee and a slice of mince pie.

"It's murder," Waring said.

"What did you learn out at Notre Dame?"

The crew from the lab were still at it, but there were signs of a struggle. Clearly Hazel Nootin had not gone gentle into that dark night. She may have been pursued across the parking lot and been caught a few feet from where the body had been found.

"Footprints?"

"Why don't we wait until I'm sure?"

"Hey, I'm not a reporter."

"You just represent the university."

Phil nodded. He had come to know the weight that the university carried in the local community. Notre Dame was the single largest employer in the area, its athletic events attracted tens of thousands of visitors every weekend, restaurants and hotels grew fat on such bounty. Accordingly, no local official lightly handled relations between city and university. It would be too much to say that there was identity of interest, but there was certainly a community of interests.

"Phil, the investigation is just beginning."

14 ⟶ HAZEL AND CHARLES NOOTIN
had married late, when he was forty-two
and she was thirty-eight. There were no children and they continued in the jobs they had when they met, she at the university
in the Center for Continuing Education, he as a private contractor. It was Hazel's first marriage, but Fig had been married
for seven years in his twenties. His first wife had died, leaving
him with two sons. It was when they were raised and off on their
own that Charles had felt free to marry again. He and Hazel
moved into a condo in one of the new developments northeast of
the university. After eight years, their marriage had achieved a
kind of equilibrium between passionate argument and equally
passionate reconciliation.

"Sometimes she said she thought I didn't regard her as my
real wife," he said to Waring and Philip, when they came to
question him.

"Why would she say that?"

"I was married before."

"Divorced?"

Charles was shocked. "I was a widower when I met Hazel.
It's not the same, getting married a second time—she was right
about that. But that didn't mean she wasn't my real wife."

"Your kids like her?"

Bernie was in the navy, and Alfred was with the Peace Corps
in the Cayman Islands. "Sure they liked her."

"Who could have done this?"

Nootin looked at Waring and at Philip. His eyes were red

and his mouth hung open. "If I knew that I wouldn't be here talking with you."

"What do you mean?"

"You know what I mean. This is twice."

"Twice?"

"This is the second time I've lost my wife."

Interviews with neighbors and friends would corroborate Nootin's admission that theirs had been a rocky marriage. "I'm no sweetheart and she could have her moods. Still, we stuck together. And that's something when there are no kids, let me tell you."

"When they weren't fighting they were making up." Verna Dopp lived in the condo next to the Nootins and some version of her remark was echoed by all the others interviewed by Philip and Waring. Could she imagine who would do such a thing?

"I think it had more to do with him than her."

"How so?" Philip asked.

"Whoever killed Hazel did it to spite Fig."

"Most murders don't require a complicated theory, Mrs. Dopp."

"You just wait and see if I'm not right."

At the University Club, Debbie suggested that the investigators talk to Karen, the manager, and Karen suggested they talk to Earl, the night bartender. Earl would have preferred not to talk at all, but Waring and Phil settled down as if they could stay until he made up his mind. That was when they learned that Fig Nootin often stopped at the club for a drink at the end of his day.

"How long did he stay?" Philip asked.

"That was the problem. He didn't want to leave once he got here."

"Was he unruly?"

"Sometimes. His wife would call."

"Ah."

"He would tell me to say he wasn't here, but she always knew I was lying," Earl explained.

"What was she like?"

Earl rubbed the tip of his nose with the back of his hand. "I don't like to judge people from what I see of them from back here. They're either better or worse than normal when they have a drink."

"Did she drink?" Waring interjected.

"Not that I know of. I guess she had lunch here now and again, but I wouldn't know about that."

"They ever here together?" Phil asked.

"When she would come for him."

"Come looking for him?"

"She always knew he was here."

"That doesn't sound like a happy relationship."

"Oh, he liked her. He wouldn't let anyone say a word against her."

"Who would have?"

"Do you know a man named Watts in Public Relations?" Waring asked.

Earl nodded. "Last night he said something about Mrs. Nootin, not realizing her husband was on the next stool. Nootin picked the guy off the stool and put him on the floor with one blow."

"Why would Watts say something about Mrs. Nootin?"

"Ask him. I don't know."

They had a drink as long as they were there, letting Earl go about his business. The club buzzed with recent events, and there was a sense of uneasiness among the waitresses. It was not a pleasant thought that a woman had met her death just a few yards from where they were working and lain there for hours undiscovered.

"I must have been only a few feet from the body when I drove away," one waitress said.

"What if she were still alive and we just drove off?" another wondered.

Phil and Waring were thinking how altered first impressions are once questioning begins. Lives are not often spoken of from such a spectator's point of view. One sensed that even for Charles his wife had become a stranger.

"Do you think he could have done it?" Waring asked.

"Could have? You and I could have." Phil had picked up this viewpoint from Roger, who rejected the notion that there is a criminal type. "Unless the class of criminals has the same extension as the class of humans." He spoke like that. Roger had taken his doctorate from Princeton in philosophy.

15

WATTS ARRIVED AS SCHEDULED
to interview Roger Knight in search of background for press releases on the coming conference with Baylor faculty.

"What happened to your face?" Roger asked. He was seated behind his desk in the chair specially constructed to support his weight.

"I cut myself shaving. Why have they got you in such a small office?"

"I was referring to the bruises."

"A man of your distinction should have a suite. Do you have a secretary?"

"I don't need a secretary," Roger said.

"This is scandalous. Did they tell you what the endowment of the Huneker Chair is?"

"If they did, I've forgotten."

"Huge," Watts said, enunciating the word and making a face to match it.

"I like this office. I chose it particularly." Watts listened skeptically while Roger told him of the convenience of parking, that he could walk the short distance to Mass at eleven-thirty upstairs or twelve-fifteen in the crypt where Orestes Brownson was buried. His frown lifted at the last remark.

"You find that proximity helps your research?"

"It is nice to know that he rests nearby."

"It is a kind of inspiration, I suppose. A communion of

minds over the grim boundary that separates the quick and the dead."

Roger realized that Watts was composing, falling naturally into the kind of prose that characterized his press releases.

"I heard you speak last night," Watts said.

"I thought I recognized you."

"Those Groucho masks fool no one."

Ten seconds went by and then Roger realized that Watts had told a joke. He was an odd duck, ducking questions about his bruised jaw. Ah well, Roger thought, it isn't any of my business. Watts added that it had been a nice crowd at the Knights of Columbus Hall.

"Then you must have heard the Reverend Edwina Marciniak?"

"Who let her in?"

"It was open to the public."

"She just wanted to disrupt the meeting. I thought you handled her well," Watts observed.

"Sometimes I wish I had the polemical skills of an Orestes Brownson. He was not a man to cross swords with unless you were prepared to battle to the death."

"Her weapon would have been the battle ax." Watts sighed. "Sometimes I wonder if women are in the same species."

"As who?"

"Us."

"Aristotle thought women were defective males, the process of gestation interrupted at a lower point. You could make the opposite case, too. Why, after all, do men have breasts? No, I think it is best to see the sexes as complementary."

"Tell it to Edwina Marciniak."

"What will be done if she tries to protest the Baylor game?"

"She'll be invisible. There will be eighty thousand fans here to see that game. Even if they notice her, they'll dismiss her for the crank she is."

"I think Brownson would have liked her."

"My estimate of the man just dropped."

Roger laughed. "I had no idea a misogynist could be gainfully employed in the present cultural climate."

"I speak confidentially, of course."

"Of course. Did you know the woman who was murdered?"

Watts shifted in his chair. "What woman?"

"Surely you've heard. Her body was found last night, near the University Club. She worked here."

"Who told you this?"

"It was on the morning news. I assumed you knew."

"Why would you assume that?" Watts sat forward and looked hard at Roger.

"Because of your function. I had thought you'd call and cancel this appointment because that news would have required your talents."

Watts settled back in his chair. "This interview is a high-priority item, as far as I'm concerned."

"But scarcely a matter of life and death."

"The Baylor game isn't that far away. Shall we get started?"

The subject of oneself is either fascinating or boring, depending. Roger had ceased to find pleasure in telling the story of his life. It did not help that Watts expected him simply to talk and did not prompt him with questions. The sound of his own voice narrating the events of his life was not conducive to cheerfulness.

"Why don't you just ask me what you'd like to know," Roger requested.

"You're doing fine."

"I am boring us both to death. What news value do you suppose an academic conference will have?"

Watts rolled his eyes upward. "I could tell you stories. Some members of the faculty think that any penny-ante thing they do has stop-the-presses importance. An economist called to tell me that he had been appointed to the board of an economics journal. He thought that should form the basis of a press release. I couldn't persuade him otherwise. So I wrote three pages, sent him a copy, and circulated it to all the local outlets. Of course they ignored it. He was positive that it was because the journal was in favor of lifting the Cuban embargo that the story had been killed."

"Surely a conference on Orestes Brownson will be of little more interest."

"You shock me. I thought you were a big fan of Orestes Brownson."

"I have no illusions about his demotic appeal," Roger stated.

"Demotic," Watts said, making a note. "I like that."

"How long have you been with the university?"

"Sometimes I feel I was born here. After graduation, I worked on a paper for a couple years and then came back."

"So you've seen a lot of changes."

"Coeducation was the big change," Watts said.

"When did that happen?"

"Nineteen seventy-two, 'seventy-three. I'd have to check."

"You were working here then?"

"No, no. I was a student."

"So you didn't really know what it had been like as an all-male institution."

"It happened when I was a junior. I enjoyed two years in Eden before the big change."

Watts seemed to have developed the persona of a chauvinist male and seized any opportunity to reenforce it. His reaction to Edwina Marciniak was perhaps understandable, but the other remarks seemed more programmatic. But surely this was not a persona that could be worn openly in the university at this time. Roger was not sure he was flattered that Watts seemed anxious to express such views to him. Did he imagine that Roger shared them?

When Watts said that he thought he had enough for his purposes, Roger had no sense of having told the public relations man much of anything. Moments after Watts left, Roger put the interview out of his mind and went back to work.

Sitting in the lower church, close to the grave of Orestes Brownson, Roger had often imagined the solemn occasion when the remains had been interred in the crypt. The great man had died in 1876, at the age of seventy-three, in Detroit, where his son lived. Buried first in Detroit, it was decided ten years later, due to the importunings of Father Sorin, to transfer the body to Notre Dame, where it would be buried in a place of honor. One might have thought this would mean burial in the community cemetery, an honor accorded to few nonmembers of the Congregation of Holy Cross, or in Cedar Grove Cemetery on Notre Dame Avenue, for all practical purposes on the campus, where such luminaries as Alexis Coquillard were buried. But for Father Sorin, to be buried in the basement of the great campus church was an honor beyond all others. There were buried one or two others, as a token of the founder's particular esteem. Orestes would join these.

The event took place ten years after his death, and was recorded in *The Scholastic* of June 19, 1886, in terms Roger came to cherish.

Last Thursday morning a solemn scene was witnessed in the church at Notre Dame when, amid the impressive rites and ceremonies with which the Christian dead are consigned to their last resting-place, the body of the late Dr. Brownson was placed in the vault which had been prepared for it underneath the sacred edifice. For the past ten years the remains of this eminent American philosopher have reposed in Mt. Eliot Cemetery at Detroit, though, about two years ago, arrangements had been made to transfer them to Notre Dame. At that time circumstances prevented the execution of the design, but on last Wednesday evening they were exhumed, and, in charge of Major Henry A. Brownson, son of the deceased philosopher, and the Rev. Aloysius Van Dyke, Rector of St. Aloysius' Church, Detroit, they were conveyed from the latter city and brought to Notre Dame, where they arrived at half-past seven o'clock next morning. They were taken to the church, escorted by a procession of the Faculty and students, headed by the University Band. A Solemn Mass of Requiem was sung by Rev. President Walsh, assisted by Fathers Zahm and Regan as deacon and subdeacon. An eloquent sermon on the life and career of the deceased Christian philosopher was delivered by Rev. S. Fitte. On the conclusion of the Mass the venerable Father General Sorin ascended the altar and spoke for a short time, alluding to his long and intimate friendship with the distinguished dead, telling how during life the lamented Christian hero had often expressed a desire to end his days at Notre Dame, and now it was their melancholy pleasure to receive his precious remains, to be placed beside other Christian heroes who had labored like him, though in other spheres of action. The final absolutions were then sung by Rev. President Walsh, after which, attended by the clergy and the relatives present, the remains were consigned to the crypt underneath the chapel—henceforth to be known as the Brownson Memorial Chapel—which forms part of the new extension of the church.

Roger had all but memorized this account. Sitting there, he liked to think of the cortege coming along Notre Dame Avenue toward Sacred Heart, students and professors accompanying it, but preceding them all the university band. What had they played as they marched solemnly along?

The sermon preached by Father Fitte, a man whose career piqued Roger's curiosity, a transplanted European who had joined the congregation after already having been ordained, lived up to the praise in *The Scholastic*. Father Walsh, the president at the time, said the requiem mass, while serving as deacon was the legendary Father Alfred Zahm, easily the most gifted member of the faculty during the first half century of the university's history. But what particularly captured Roger's fancy was the thought of the venerable founder himself, Father Sorin, speaking of his old friend from the altar steps. The peroration of the article was striking:

> And so sleeps the great Dr. Brownson amid the peaceful shades of Notre Dame, for which he had in life entertained the warmest feelings, and in whose works he had often taken the deepest interest and to the advancement of which he himself contributed in no slight degree. The desire which in life could not be gratified, that he should close his life's work in this spot of earth, now finds its partial realization in that the place of his choice is made the privileged home of the treasured remains of that frame which once embodied a soul so grand and so good. May the student of Notre Dame, for years to come, find herein a constant reminder of a noble example in the performance of life's duties, through the right employment of God-given talent and genius in the service of religion, humanity, and country—and example of unswerving fidelity to truth and principle—such as is presented in the life and career of Dr. Orestes A. Brownson.

Written by an anonymous student, presumably one of the staff—Dexter, Hagenbarth, Goulding, Cleary, or Mulkern—the account contained not a hint of irony. Had subsequent generations of students taken a cue from the great man? Whatever the case, the current generation was totally unaware of him and Roger took pleasure in the thought that in some small way he might alter that and return the name of Orestes Brownson to a position of honor among the students.

What circumstances, he wondered, had caused a ten-year

delay in executing the decision to bring the body of Brownson to Notre Dame? He must see if there was anything in the archives that might throw light on that question.

"Have a good day?" Philip asked when he came by for him at five-thirty.

Roger had to think, and then he remembered his interview with Watts. He gave Philip a glum account of it.

"Watts? Did you talk about Hazel Nootin?"

"The woman found dead? Watts hadn't heard the news yet."

"He hadn't?"

"You seem surprised."

"I suppose he wouldn't have told you of his troubles with her over the conference you're taking part in."

"What kind of troubles?"

"Apparently she was a difficult person to work with. At least Watts thought so. He had been grousing about her to Earl the bartender at the faculty club. Called her a nasty name. Unfortunately for him, Charles Nootin was sitting on the next stool."

"He struck him?"

"I thought you hadn't heard this."

"I saw the bruise on his jaw."

"Funny he didn't mention any of that."

"Did Fig Nootin?"

Phil looked at his brother and smiled. "No. As a matter of fact he didn't."

"I suppose he gets credit for gallantry."

The Knights knew Fig in his professional capacity, as he had been engaged to line the walls of their apartment with shelves for Roger's books. Roger had wanted boards and bricks, anything that would enable him to get his books out of boxes and up where he could see their familiar bindings. Fig Nootin had shaken his head.

"Not in these rooms. You want something nice."

He sketched what he proposed on a sheet of paper. He measured, he figured, and, when he named his price, Roger told him to go ahead. And go ahead he did, more or less. He worked at his own pace. Some days he was busy at home, sawing, staining, pegging; other days he was installing the result in the apartment. On yet other days—the majority—he was nowhere to be found. It was risky to be at home while Fig was there, as he liked to pump Roger about what he was doing at his computer.

"I ought to get one of those."

"You can get a pretty good one out at the mall," Roger told Fig.

"My sons communicate with one another by computer."

"E-mail."

"Yeah."

Nootin went on to talk about his sons, Bernie and Alfred, and of their mother, who had died so young. Roger began to think of Nootin's sons as younger versions of Phil and himself.

"Did they find it easy to adjust to their new mother?"

"Don't ever call her that. Hazel isn't their mother—she's my wife."

Roger, sensing this was a delicate topic, let it go. Nootin was already onto something else.

"What are you teaching, Professor?"

"It's hard to tell until I give an exam."

"I never went to college."

"Anyone who can make shelves like those is better off making shelves like those."

Nootin got the hint and returned to work.

16

EDWINA PICKED UP HER TELE-
phone and made a call to the editor of the
South Bend Tribune. Of course they were reluctant to put her
through, but mentioning that she was pastor of a downtown
church proved to be an open-sesame. She was asked to hold.
After a few minutes, the girl came on again. "I'm sorry. I didn't
get your name."

"Reverend Marciniak."

"And you are pastor of—"

"Is it regular practice for the *Tribune* to grill subscribers
who wish to have a word with the editor?"

"Hello, hello," a male voice broke in. "This is Harry Men-
dax. Can I help you?"

"Are you the editor?"

"I am one of the editors, yes."

Edwina sighed in resignation. "I would like to make a comment on the murder that took place on the campus of the University of Notre Dame. The victim was not known to me, but
perhaps that is just as well, for her death is significant beyond her
personal tragedy." Edwina paused. "Are you getting all this?"

"Thank you for expressing your views."

"I have hardly begun."

"If you would leave your number, we will call you in the
event that we decide to do a feature on this story."

"Do you intend to ignore it?" Edwina demanded.

The line seemed to have gone dead. Edwina pressed the re-
dial button and was rewarded with a busy signal. She slammed

down the phone. She wanted a bully pulpit and all she had was her own pulpit and this was midweek. Oh, how frustrating to have an event like this with which to pummel and punish the Catholic Church and to get the runaround from the only local paper. Of course the *Tribune* would not antagonize Notre Dame. The local police would not antagonize Notre Dame. And underlying it all was Edwina's deep resentment that Baylor University had consented to play a football game at Notre Dame.

"Consented?" that idiot Watts had replied when she voiced this sentiment the night before at the talk in the residence hall on campus. "They've begged for years to play here. It doesn't matter if they lose. It will make their season."

Edwina had put away any interest in athletics when she abjured her childhood faith. Both had characterized her family, and to repudiate one was to repudiate the other. Once, she had been able to rattle off sports statistics as rapidly as any of her cousins. Yes, Notre Dame records had been part of her repertoire. It shamed her now to think how she had rhapsodized over Rockne, lauded Leahy, praised Parseghian, deified Devine, and sung hosannahs to Holtz. No wonder Watts's wise-guy remark hit home. She sensed the truth in what he said. The premier Baptist university in the land cavorted with the whore of Babylon for thirty pieces of silver. Had they no pride? Was everyone bamboozled by Catholic efforts to conceal how they had eclipsed the ancient faith with unforgivable additions?

New as she herself was to the ranks of Protestantism, Edwina sometimes felt that she alone had some semblance of the passion with which the reformers had attacked Rome. What would Martin Luther say to the mamby-pamby accommodationists who had the gall to invoke his name? What would Calvin say of those who blinked at papist blasphemy in the name of ecumenism? Edwina felt like a Crusader determined to take back the holy faith from the infidels. Must she fight this battle alone? There had been no offers of solidarity once she announced her intention to obstruct the Baylor–Notre Dame game.

90

She opened the yellow pages to "Churches" and ran her finger down the list of Baptist churches, choosing one at random, a church in the suburbs. Telephone the pastor? Edwina shook away the idea. She would drive out there and talk to the pastor, Webster Stone, eye to eye.

For whatever reason, Edwina would not have associated the Baptist Church with suburbia. Consequently, the sight of Hope Baptist was a revelation. Surrounded by acres of blacktop parking lots, the brick mass of the church rose commandingly from a level terrain. On the marquee over the door was the title of next Sunday's sermon: THE GREEN WOOD AND THE DRY.

A two-story wing jutted out from the church: the school. A matching wing on the other side contained offices. Half a dozen cars were parked there. Edwina added her four-wheeler to them and strode toward a pair of glass doors. They slid open automatically as she approached and she was admitted to a carpeted hallway with walls of soft color and indirect lighting. There was a building directory in the vestibule as well as a floor plan. "You Are Here." Well, she already knew that. Her eye picked out Pastor's Study and she planned her journey into this terra incognita.

Pastor Webster Stone looked up through wire-rimmed trifocals, his smile forming as he did. It hesitated a third of the way along when he got a good look at the woman who had banged imperiously on his open door. It was his boast that he could tell a fellow Baptist at a hundred yards, but in the case of the little lady in the doorway he would have been certain at half a mile that she was not one.

"Good day, madam."

Edwina strode toward the desk and thrust out her hand. Involuntarily, Webster threw up his hands, and for a wild moment he thought robbery and sacrilege were about to be committed.

"The Reverend Edwina Marciniak."

"No ma'am. Webster Stone."

"I am identifying myself. I am a fellow wearer of the cloth. I am pastor of the Independent Protestant Church of Jesus Christ and His Almighty Parent."

There are some who can disguise their shock and distaste when confronted with the unthinkable, but Webster Stone was not among them. With intimates he had expressed himself in firm biblical tones on the matter of a woman speaking in church, let alone from the pulpit. Others might twist passages from Acts all they like and find in Paul's greeting to this church or that warrant for the belief that a woman as well as a man could preach the Gospel. Webster had set his face sternly against such nonsense.

"What do you think of celibacy, Web?" they kidded him.

"As little as possible."

"Next thing you'll be using incense," the kidders would say, or "What's this I hear about vestments at Hope Baptist?"

Such diversionary tactics were not worthy of response. On other matters, perhaps, Webster was vulnerable to the charge of being soft on Rome, on matters of pro-life, but then all these kidders would agree with him there.

"What do the Baptist pastors intend to do about the game Baylor has scheduled with Notre Dame?"

"Go to it, madam. Cheer on old Baylor and hope that victory is snatched from the jaws of almost certain defeat."

Edwina let out an anguished cry and collapsed into a chair. "I do not believe my ears."

"Are you ill?"

Webster was more puzzled by his visitor now than he had been when she claimed to be a pastor. Thank God she did not claim to be a Baptist. But here she was, apparently on a mission to tell Baptist pastors how to be good Baptists. She made this perfectly clear.

"Baptist pastors have to speak out against this outrage. Don't you realize what this game will mean to the nation?"

92

"I know what it will mean to Baylor."

"Of course you do. It will discredit the school in the eyes of simple believers whose faith is based on their Bible and who know what to think of the Church of Rome."

"It's a football game," Webster said, incredulous.

"Bread and circuses, Pastor Stone. Bread and circuses."

"What is your interest in the matter?"

"The only interest that a conscientious Protestant can have. I intend to protest this outrage, to speak against it, to stop it if possible. Are you telling me that I must stand alone?"

"How much do you know of the Baptist Church, madam?" asked Webster.

"Stop calling me madam."

"Very well." He would not call her reverend or pastor.

"What I know of the Baptist Church is that it is Protestant. What more need I know? That is what Baylor seems to have forgotten. I do not want to believe that the Baptist pastors in this area have similarly forgotten their opposition to Rome."

"I believe you mentioned an independent Protestant church. The phrase might well describe us Baptists. We have no central body that dictates policy for the rest of us. There are loose confederations, meetings, of course, and there is at least a family resemblance between one church and another. You speak of local Baptist pastors. There are indeed local Baptist pastors and in good number. But I do not speak for them and they do not speak for me."

"You suggested that you all intended to go to the football game."

Webster had been contacted by both Baylor and Notre Dame on the matter of tickets. Of course he had bought tickets that would place him on the Baylor side of the field. He soon learned that the other Baptist pastors had received identical offers and that to a man they had eagerly grasped the opportunity to buy tickets. But these were individual decisions, arrived at individually. He painstakingly pointed this out to his frowning visitor, wondering why he was doing so. If he was not accountable to another Baptist in the way she imagined, he certainly was not accountable to her.

"Very well. Why do you yourself exhibit this strange desire to dance to the tune of the Church of Rome?"

"Football is not a Catholic game."

"But you are playing the Catholic game by going to that stadium. Ever since their alleged ecumenical council they have been hard at work smudging the differences between their baroque excresences and the true Christian faith. They would have us believe that we are all secretly Catholic."

"Oh, I very much doubt that."

"Then you have not read *Lumen Gentium.*"

"I don't read Latin."

"You can read it in translation. Know your enemy."

There are limits even to Baptist patience. Webster Stone had had just about enough of this scolding; he might have been back in school having a surprise quiz sprung on him. He felt an overwhelming desire not only to respond to this woman, but to shock her.

"As far as that goes, the Roman Church has stood rock firm on the matter of abortion. I am not alone in admiring their valiant pope for speaking Christian truth when all around it is being mocked. I have come to think that we should take more seriously what they say about contraception. The Catholics are our powerful allies in the defense of family values."

Edwina's pudgy hand went to her pudgy breast and a great cry came from her: *"Eloi, Eloi, lama sabachtana."*

"You are being sacrilegious."

"Sacrilegious!" Her breath was coming in short gasps.

"Applying our Lord's words to yourself! You are a fine one to come here and presume to instruct me in how to be a Baptist. You are a perfect example of why the Lord forbade women to speak out in church."

Edwina staggered to her feet, looking wildly at Webster Stone, who had risen to his full six foot seven and seemed about to drive her from the temple. She fled. She left the room and staggered down the hallway. People were emerging from doorways and staring at the fleeing Edwina.

"Go," Webster Stone said, emerging from his office and striking a stance. He lifted a hand and pointed. "Go, woman, and sin no more."

17
running out of the church door out of control, and Elijah Phipps caught her out of self-protection rather than anything else, and with a gentleness that belied his size. She turned in his arms, looked up at him with wide, terrified eyes, and tried to form a word. It seemed to be "Rape." Her eyes rolled upward and she was limp in his arms. Paster Webster Stone now stood in the doorway.

"Who is she, Preacher?" Elijah asked.

"It's a long story."

"What should I do with her?"

Stone heaved a sigh of Christian resignation. "Bring her inside, I guess."

Elijah lifted the little woman as if she were a rag doll and followed Webster Stone inside. He settled his burden on a couch, straightened, and took a deep breath of the bracing Baptist air of the church center. Women from other offices came to attend to the fallen woman. Water was brought, and cold cloths. In a moment she came sputtering awake and looked wildly around. When her eyes came to Elijah, it seemed she might faint again.

"Elijah, this is the Reverend Edwina Marciniak."

"Ha."

"Did you laugh at me?"

"No, ma'am."

A lady preacher might be a possibility some places, but not down in Bristlo, Texas, where Elijah Samuel Phipps had been raised, dirt poor on a dirt-poor farm on the edge of a town that was flat on flat. Off in the distance around Austin, the earth rose a little to form itself into a species of hills, but in Bristlo everything was level—geographically, morally, socially. Elijah was seven years old before he realized he was black, as in nonwhite. That was at school. In the Baptist church they went to everyone was black and no mention was made of the fact that there were other races. He hadn't yet realized that there were other parts of town than the one in which he lived with white people in them.

School had changed that. Elijah had been struck dumb by all those pale faces. The first day he ran his hand over the face of a girl with little spots and hair like carrots and she screamed. After that, Elijah hardly made a move for three years, just sitting quiet, keeping his mouth shut, wondering why the teacher explained everything so many times. It was in about his third year that his mother and father were told by a teacher that Elijah's scores were high.

"That boy's smart or he cheats good 'cause I've never caught him at it." The teacher was built straight up and down with no meat on her and hair parted in the middle and great big thick glasses: Mrs. Sprocket.

"Elijah don't cheat." His father would say that just once, so Mrs. Sprocket better be careful.

"Then he's smart."

"We already know that."

"You sure about his age?"

"What you mean?"

"He's big."

"We Phippses is all big."

Elijah had been struck by how small all his classmates were. They didn't like the fact that he found school easy, but they wanted him on their side in games. The first baseball Elijah hit went up like a rocket and came down way off in a puff of dust. He could kick a football at least as far. By the time he entered high school, everyone in Bristlo knew he was a natural athlete.

"What you want to be, Elijah?"

"A preacher."

Elijah knew his Bible. It had been read to him before he could read it himself. It was the book on which he learned to read. It was the only book in the house, but what more do you need than *the* book? In Sunday school, Elijah found that he had already gotten great chunks of the book by heart. He ran away with ribbons time and again, and when he sat in church, his mother at one end of the seat, his father at the other, and all the kids in between, Elijah hung on the words of the preacher. He imagined himself up there, holding that Bible open in the palm of his hand, sweat running down his face, his voice rising and falling, now loud, now soft, his whole body like a musical instrument singing the praises of the Lord.

He made the first team in football as a freshman, and that's when real attention began to be paid to Elijah Samuel Phipps. He began on the line, he was switched to the backfield, he was tried at quarterback and seemed made for the position. He had an uncanny ability to read defenses, which was not that hard in high school maybe, but people began to call him ESP.

They said Elijah Samuel Phipps had some kind of natural radar. He was never sacked, and he threw balls where no one was and suddenly there was his receiver. If a play did not develop, he ran the ball himself. He was all-state in a state where competition is fierce. Earnest men in neckties came to talk to his parents.

They wanted him to come to college. To play ball. It was a bonus that his grade point average was good. At seventeen years old, Elijah faced an embarrassment of choices. But from the time Baylor offered him a scholarship, Elijah's mind was made up. A Baptist school! He felt it was his duty to play football there. And then the Notre Dame coach sat down with his father.

"Mr. Phipps, your son has an excellent academic record."

"He's done good."

"Some places might not care about his mind, but Notre Dame wants scholar athletes. Elijah would get an excellent education."

"How cold is it up there?" his mother asked.

"Winters are rough."

They had television now and Elijah had watched the Bears and Green Bay play in weather he had never seen. Snow. The very word had a mystical sound to it, as if the one saying it were expressing disbelief that there could be anything so wonderful.

"Of course our athletes get national coverage every game. Every game."

They had watched Notre Dame, always rooting for the opponent. No one had mentioned the word *Catholic* yet.

"We're Baptists," Elijah had said to the coach.

"I know that. There have always been Protestants at Notre Dame. Always. From the very beginning." He mentioned a tight end who had been a runner-up for the Heisman the year before. "A Methodist. And of course there is Joe Thiesmann himself."

Be polite, hear him out, he was a nice man, Elijah's manners told him, but his mind was made up. He had a call to Baylor and he could not refuse the Lord.

"Notre Dame sounds pretty good," his father said later.

"I liked that coach," his mother said. "Why, he's not Catholic himself."

His father said, "Of course it's cold up there."

Visions of snow falling like manna from heaven clouded Elijah's mind. Baylor got buried in drifts of it. The call became fainter. He found himself agreeing with his father that the only sensible thing was to go to Notre Dame.

Decisions are strange. Elijah would have thought it was like going up the street to the corner and then you either went left or right or straight ahead. Simple. But the decision to go to Notre Dame was not like that. It was as if they had already decided and it was just a matter of realizing that the choice had already been made. The next August Elijah went to Austin and got on a plane, and a few hours later he was in South Bend, Indiana.

His first impression was that it was beautiful. The fields were full of corn, everything was green, and there were hills and lakes—why, just seven miles to the north was Lake Michigan, as big as any ocean, and all around in the country there were lakes ringed by cottages. There were even two lakes on the campus of Notre Dame.

Elijah got his first glimpse of the golden dome from the air, and the pilot said that was a statue of Knute Rockne up there on top, but Elijah knew who she was. That's what Notre Dame meant. Did his mother and father know that? He had never asked. Looking down at the campus and at that dome, Elijah thought it looked like the land of Egypt, and he was going to go down there and live among the fleshpots and what would become of him?

He got settled in and practice began and he located Hope Baptist and telephoned and explained who he was and Pastor Webster Stone said he would have a van swing by campus to pick up Elijah the next Sunday morning. Hope Baptist turned out not to be exactly what he expected, and for a time he thought of trying a more modest church, but Pastor Stone was so welcoming and all the brothers and sisters, too, and they were all Notre Dame fans. Somehow that made things all right, and Elijah's Notre Dame career began.

He liked his classes, he liked the campus, he liked playing football in a program that had a tradition like no other. Two years had gone by with less than perfect success for the team, but Elijah gained national fame. ESP became ESPN, except on NBC, which carried all the home games. Every chance he got, Elijah told the writers that his mother wished they would call him Elijah and sometimes they did, but most of the time it was ESPN.

Elijah could remember his reaction the first time he realized that Notre Dame was scheduled to play Baylor on October 31,

1998. A chill went through him. He felt as the Israelites must have felt when the Lord told them how they had strayed from righteousness and were living like strangers in a strange land. How could he play against Baylor? He felt he had a conflict of interest. But no one seemed to understand. Not even Pastor Stone.

"Baylor's come along," Pastor Stone said. "But they're not in the same league as Notre Dame."

"It's a Baptist school."

"What are you getting at?"

"Notre Dame is Catholic."

"This is football," retorted the pastor.

There was no point in Elijah's saying that he felt he had sold his inheritance for a mess of pottage. The blessing that would have been his if he had gone to Baylor had descended on someone else. His very success at Notre Dame seemed a judgment on him. Elijah would wake in the night and listen, as if the Lord had called and had something to say to him. But there were only night sounds and the thumping of his own heart. He lost sleep. His appetite was not what it should have been. He found himself daydreaming in class. He had determined to talk it out again with Pastor Stone.

That was why he had been coming from his car when the stubby little lady came careening out the door and barreled right into him, screamed, and fainted. Now she said she was a preacher.

"Not Baptist," Webster Stone said, trying to keep his voice level.

"Independent Protestant," she barked. "With the accent on *Protestant.*"

"Elijah is on the Notre Dame football team," Pastor Stone said proudly.

She had gotten to her feet, but now she stepped back. "Are you Catholic?"

"No, ma'am."

"Praise God. What are you doing playing for that heathen institution?"

"It's a Catholic school."

"Then you do know that. Explain yourself."

Webster Stone intervened and the little woman was led away. Elijah watched her being convoyed down the corridor and outside, her voice going a mile a minute.

What she had said had pierced his very soul.

18

AGATHA HAD WATCHED EDwina's intervention at Professor Roger Knight's talk in the Knights of Columbus Hall. It was clear that her cousin wished to debate the lecturer, but it was also clear that the lecturer took seriously what she said. It was an odd feeling that her cousin, who had so publicly left the Church, obviously knew more about its teachings than she or most of the other kids at the talk. Yet she seemed to think their heads had been poured full of Catholic propaganda.

"Of course I have," Nicholas answered when she asked him if he had read the document Edwina referred to.

"When?"

"Last semester. I told you I took a course from him."

"I've never read it. I'm not sure I ever heard of it before."

"We could read it together if you'd like."

Well, it was a different approach. But she was still trying to avoid Howard, her fellow cheerleader with whom she refused to team anymore. There are certain acrobatic feats where a male cheerleader hoists his female partner high above his head, supporting her in a manner that, in any other circumstance, would earn him a slap on the face. Agatha had never known any other cheerleaders to treat such performances as anything but impersonal and professional. But Howard had apparently read into their joint performance a pledge of intimacy. The one time she had gone out with him he seemed to want to continue in private what had been done in public. She had slapped his face. He had grabbed her wrist and pulled her to him. His expression was a frightening combination of anger and lust. He'd pressed his lips to hers. She bit his mouth and he cried out in pain, but his grip loosened. When he lunged at her again, she had raised her knee and disabled him. By all rights he should have been mad enough to kill her. But, on reflection, he had come to consider the episode as proof that they were destined for one another. Nicholas was not just any port in a storm, but she had the sense that she was using him. But what could be more innocent than reading together a document from Vatican II?

Agatha learned of the murder of the woman who had worked on campus through a phone call from Edwina.

"Agatha? Edwina."

She swam slowly upward toward the surface and consciousness. When she realized who was on the phone, she began to babble about how well Edwina had done the night before.

"Well! I hardly got a word in. Have you heard of this poor woman?"

"What woman?"

"It was on the morning news."

"I'm just getting up," Agatha said.

"It is going on ten o'clock."

"I have no morning class."

Edwina sputtered in disapproval. "A woman's dead body has been found on the campus there. I am calling to make certain you are all right."

"Of course I'm all right."

"It is the least your parents would expect of me, to ascertain your safety when dead bodies are being found all over the Notre Dame campus."

"How many bodies?"

"Did you hear that man last night, going on about some bones buried in the basement of the church there? I suppose he expects you to worship them."

"Orestes Brownson."

"None of you seemed to know who he was," Edwina said.

"Did you?"

"Of course."

"I never heard of him before," Agatha admitted.

"That is no loss, although I must say I am surprised. He was a great trophy when he lost his mind and faith and became a Catholic."

"Edwina, all your relatives are Catholics. You used to be a Catholic."

"If I had an hour to talk to you woman-to-woman, you would soon see the wisdom of what I have done. You would follow in my footsteps."

"Oh, I doubt that. What about the dead woman?"

"You can get the details from television and newspaper. Of course it will be a distorted version. But I am sure you have mind enough to pierce through the lies to see what really happened."

"What really happened?"

"We may never know."

On this enigmatic note the conversation ended. Agatha was fully awake now. She took a shower and was even more awake. And ravenously hungry. The phone rang again.

"This is Nicholas. Am I right in thinking you have no class this morning?"

"I just got up."

"Let's have breakfast."

They agreed to meet in the Huddle, the fast-food eatery in the student center. Nicholas was already at a table with a tray heaped high with hamburgers, french fries, and soft drinks.

"That's breakfast?"

"Actually, I already had breakfast."

"I want a cup of coffee."

"Sit down. I'll get it for you."

"No." She laughed, but it was a nice gesture. When she was returning to the table with coffee and rolls, Howard stood in her path, a great, many-toothed smile on his face.

"Can I join you?"

"I'm with someone."

"Anyone I know?"

"I doubt it. Let me by."

"Is something the matter?" This was from Nicholas, who had crossed the room to see what was going on. Agatha's manner had suggested that something was amiss. Howard turned to look at Nicholas, who came up to about his upper arm.

"Who are you?"

Nicholas ignored him, took Agatha's tray, and told her to follow him. A second later, the tray was flying in the air and Nicholas was standing open mouthed, looking at it.

"Oh, I'm sorry," Howard said. "What have I done!"

Nicholas deftly caught the descending tray and in a single motion brought it down on Howard's head. There was a dull *bong*. And then Howard had both of Nicholas's wrists in his grip. He applied pressure and Nicholas yelped in pain and he was forced to his knees. Perhaps it was association of ideas. Perhaps it was the kind of memory one's limbs took on to perform acrobatics. Agatha lifted her knee and Howard cried out in pain, his face went white, and he staggered backward into a table, which did not support him but began to slide. He ended up on the floor, groaning in acute pain.

"I'll have some of your hamburger," Agatha said.

"Would you like me to get you another cup of coffee?"

"I'll have some of your Coke."

They stepped over Howard and returned to their table.

"Who was he?"

"He asked the same thing about you."

"You don't have to tell me."

"He's a cheerleader. A real airhead." She pulled her chair up to the table. "He hasn't even read—what's the name of the document we're going to read?"

"Lumen Gentium."

She repeated the words, finding them good.

"They found a dead woman on campus," Nicholas said. He was watching Howard hobble from the room, looking back murderously at the two who had humbled him. Agatha would have dropped out of cheerleading then and there, but why should she do that? It was a small but significant step toward her Hannah Storm goal.

"Edwina called to tell me that."

"Is she really your cousin?"

"Unless the gypsies substituted her in my cousin's crib."

"She sounded angry."

"She lost her faith and became a Protestant and now she has a church downtown. She wants to stop the Baylor game."

"What is she, a big Baylor fan?"

"She thinks it's a scandal for Protestants to come here and play football."

"She sounds nuts."

"She's smart. She's read *Lumen Gentium.* She called to find out if I was safe, pretending that women were lying dead all over the campus."

Nicholas seemed to know all about it. Hazel Nootin had worked at the Center for Continuing Education.

"The building next to the post office? I've never been there. I can count the times I've been in the post office."

"They put on conferences. She was a program director. The body was found in front of the University Club."

"I've been there."

When her family was down for a game last fall, they had eaten afterward in the club. It had been crowded and chaotic and gloomy since Notre Dame had lost the game, but all the Marciniaks took heart as the time of the end of the game receded and they stoked up on beer.

"To think it happened just last night," Nicholas said.

The night of the talk. Afterward, she had stayed around and

watched Nicholas enjoy his triumph. She had felt a bit like a trophy, the way he insisted on introducing her to everybody. The chaplain seemed surprised to learn that she was a cheerleader.

"Do you go to games?" he had asked Nicholas.

"Is the pope Polish?"

"I am," Agatha said. This seemed to surprise Nicholas. "What did you think Marciniak was?" she had teased.

"A pseudonym. No, I'm kidding. I knew all along. I myself am Aleut."

"What's that?"

Nicholas had sighed. "The same old story. No one remembers."

He was kidding. If Agatha saw that, Father Grosseteste had not, insisting that Nicholas explain what an Aleut was.

"The Aleutian Islands, Father," Nicholas had told him.

"Where are they?"

"Off the African coast."

Agatha had turned away, lest the priest see her laugh. Nicholas was a nut, but he was fun. He said he would walk her back to her hall and she had agreed, and they'd walked under the rustling trees with a wind high above that did not affect them at ground level. It would have been spooky to walk alone at that hour. Not that she felt unsafe on campus. Now, in the daylight familiarity of the Huddle, she thought that it might have been while they were strolling along that the woman was being assaulted outside the University Club and left for dead.

19 ALL THE WHILE HE WAS INTER-
viewing Roger Knight, Watts was trying to push from his mind the events of the previous evening. He took comfort from the fact that he had been seen at the lecture, not least by the lecturer himself. From there he had driven home. The prospect of another drink was oddly unattractive. When he left the faculty club earlier, he had gone to the Linebacker and had a couple more drinks. Just to prove to himself that he could handle it. He sat at the bar with his sore jaw in his hand and managed to escape intrusive questions. He had gone from the bar back to campus and the Knights of Columbus Hall for the talk.

He realized that he was preparing himself for the inquiries that would surely come. Had it been wise to pretend to Knight that he had not heard of the death of Hazel Nootin?

Hazel Nootin. She might be dead, but her name still evoked vindictive thoughts. He found himself thinking that she had gotten just what she deserved. It was a grim thought, a woman lying out in the night dead, but any death is grim. When he got to his campus office, he listened to the radio news. The victim's husband, his hairy son at his side, was described as in a state of despondency.

"He is being questioned about the details of these events."

Watts felt the leap of hope. What a parlay that would be, Hazel and Hazel's husband knocked off like a combination shot in billiards. He actually hummed as he crossed the campus on his way to Knight's office. When he got to Brownson Hall, he was sure he had misunderstood. A sign told him that offices of adjunct and junior faculty could be found by descending the stairway at the side of the building. To his left, through the trees, was the grotto, and then, cranking round to the right, the road that led on between the lakes, passed the community cemetery, and continued to St. Mary's College across the highway. To the right of that was a parking lot. Watts remembered when it had been a laundry, St. Michael's Laundry. It had burned down, as so many campus buildings had during the first fifty years of the school, and, rather than being rebuilt there, had been moved out beyond the credit union, across Douglas Road. Descending the stairway, Watts passed the offices of Sacred Heart parish, then stopped, again unable to believe that a distinguished professor had been assigned offices in this out-of-the-way place. Decio was not much, in Watts's estimation, but this was like putting him up in Old College. He found the entrance and went along a crooked passage to the door on which was taped a piece of paper lettered with ROGER KNIGHT. To such disfavor the Huneker Professor of Catholic Studies had come.

Roger Knight was happy as a lark in what he called his digs. A massive computer had been installed and a chair ample enough to receive his considerable bottom. To his credit, he seemed loath to speak about himself, and what he did say was already contained in the Knight dossier in Watts's office.

The interview over, Watts returned to his office to be told that two gentlemen were waiting for him. One was a South Bend police detective named Waring and the other introduced himself as Philip Knight.

"Knight."

"Mr. Knight is a private investigator hired by the university."

"We already have one Knight working here."

"My brother, Roger."

"Obviously not twins," Watts observed.

"We want to ask you a few questions about your relations with the deceased, Hazel Nootin," Waring said.

"Take a pew," Watts said, making an expansive gesture. He himself went around his desk, striking his thigh on its corner as he did. He yelped and limped to his chair. Throwing himself into it, he set it rolling but was saved by the wall. The impact pitched him slightly forward. His two visitors watched all this with some apprehension.

"You all right?" Phil asked.

"I'm fine. I wasn't related to Hazel Nootin."

"But you knew her."

"Of course. It's my job to know people throughout the university."

"Did you know her husband?"

Watts's hand went to his jaw. Obviously Earl had told all.

"The poor fellow," Watts said, shaking his head.

"One of his sons is home and the other may get compassionate leave from his ship."

Watts liked Philip Knight's apparent interpretation of his remark: grief for the new widower. Actually, he had been thinking of being married to Hazel. But from what he had seen of Fig, they probably deserved one another.

"Is it true that he struck you at the University Club last night?" Waring said.

"A violent man." Watts paused and his brows rose above his glasses. "Aha."

"You've thought of something?"

"I see the line you're pursuing. Of course it can be said that I gave him provocation—unwittingly, let me add. I commented on his wife and he went bananas. But I suppose Earl told you all that."

"Something like that," Waring said.

"Did she come for him?"

"Who?"

"Nootin's wife. Earl told me she often came to drag him away from the club."

Whatever uneasiness Watts had felt at the sight of his visitors was gone. He felt like a good citizen helping the police do their work.

"Did you say the university has hired you, Mr. Knight?"

"They have, yes," Phil replied.

"Wise move. Not that the police aren't more than competent. But this impinges on my area. The reputation of an institution is a delicate thing. Years of contributions and success can go up in smoke in a minute as a result of one terrible event. Do you think Nootin is responsible for the death of his wife?"

"Do you?"

"I?" Watts laid a splayed hand on his breast. "I haven't any idea."

"What was she like?" Phil said.

He put out his hand and moved some objects about on the surface of his desk. How to put this? "Does the name Xanthippe mean anything to you?"

"Sam who?" Waring asked.

"Roger would know," Phil said.

"She was Socrates' wife."

Waring clearly had as much trouble with Socrates as he'd had with Xanthippe.

"She was a fishwife. A harridan. The scourge of all and sundry. She was tyrannical, whimsical, unpredictable. To work with her was to have a foretaste of hell."

"Did you work with her?"

Watts now addressed Philip Knight. "You know of the conference your brother will take part in a few days before the Baylor game? She is the program director. She has reduced Austin Schwartz to a neurotic mess."

"Gave him a hard time?"

"He can tell you all about it."

"Austin Schwartz?"

Watts pulled out a campus directory and handed it across the desk to Waring. "You can use my phone, if you'd like."

------▶

Almost as soon as the door closed behind them, it opened again and Fenwick slipped in. His face was a mask of anticipation, and he actually tiptoed to Watts's desk, his finger pressed against his lips.

"What did they want?" he whispered.

"Sit down," Watts said with resignation. "Obviously I am not going to get much work done today."

Fenwick sat on the edge of the chair and leaned toward Watts. "Well?"

"I told them they could find anything I knew in the personnel files."

"Like what?" Fenwick said.

"Of course I think they should talk directly to you, but there was something about legal representation and not wanting to jeopardize their case."

Fenwick fell back in his chair. "What are you saying?"

"Relax. I told them nothing. How could I? I don't know how you spend your evenings."

For twenty minutes, Watts toyed with Fenwick as a cat toys with a ball of yarn. Telling Fenwick that his visitors had not asked about him directly, that in fact his name had never been pronounced, only convinced Fenwick that he had been the object of the visitation.

"What in God's name do they think?"

"Had you known Hazel Nootin? Had you worked with her? I suppose they'll discover that your wife has left you," Watts speculated.

"Left me! She's visiting her mother in Peoria," Fenwick insisted.

"Of course."

"It's true."

"I'll back you all the way."

"Do you have anything to drink?"

Watts brought his hands together in prayer and rolled his eyes to heaven. Fenwick left. In the bottom drawer of his desk, right side, there was a pint of brandy, aspirin, Tylenol, cold tablets, breath freshener, and gum. The present occasion seemed to call for brandy. Having opened it, Watts brought the bottle to his nose and inhaled deeply. Then he put it to his lips, tipped back his head, and took his medicine.

20   GOD CAN BRING GOOD EVEN
out of evil. Austin Schwartz repeated this
home truth to himself, trying to repress a smile. What was that
scene in *I, Claudius* when the exiled Tiberius learns from a
somber legate that Augustus is dead and breaks into uncontrol-
lable laughter? That historic scene paled to insignificance compared with the sense of relief Austin felt at the realization that
Hazel Nootin would not be there to kick him around anymore.
Her unexpected demise on the lawn outside the University Club
might have been the sort of thing the nuns had meant all those
years ago: God can bring good even out of evil.

Schwartz loped across the campus, making a kind of
whistling noise. He grinned at passing students, tossed a glance
of thanksgiving at the great gilt statue of Our Lady atop the
golden dome. Austin Schwartz was not a religious man, superfi-
cially. Way deep down, at the core of his soul, the beliefs of his
childhood and youth were still archived, but practice had become desultory with the years and with the bewildering changes
in the Church. Religion had become a professional expertise,
what he talked about in classes, gave papers about at the meetings of various scholarly societies. Before now, it had been years
since he had felt an impulse to drop to his knees and cry out,
"Deo gratias!" The fact that the phrase came to him in Latin indicated when he had dropped out of the liturgical loop.

He was on his way to a meeting with Pickle the assistant
provost, called to insure that recent tragic events would not jeopardize the academic conference that would be held in the week

prior to the Baylor game. Schwartz was given a seat, and the wiry administrator paced back and forth across his office, moving in a Groucho crouch, nervous as a cat.

"You know the game is on Reformation Day," Pickle said.

"Did anyone realize that when it was scheduled?"

"Ha. Certainly nobody here." He brought a hand to his mouth as if to erase what he had said. "So far as I know. Have you seen this morning's paper?"

"The *Times?*"

Pickle moved his head and looked at him with narrowed eyes. "The *South Bend Tribune.* I don't know how many complaints I've received about McGough. A sportswriter. Apparently he failed to make the team at Valparaiso, became a journalist, and has dedicated himself to savaging Notre Dame. Look at this."

Pickle whipped a paper from his desk and thrust it under Schwartz's nose. ND TO NAIL BAYLOR TO DOOR ON REFORMATION DAY. Schwartz scanned the article quickly. McGough belonged to the metaphorical school of sportswriters; forced analogies and similies studded his prose. But even a literal mind might have found significance in the fact that the great Catholic university Notre Dame was scheduled to engage in battle with Baylor, the Baptist institution par excellence, on Reformation Day. McGough gave an excited word picture of the Baylor coaching staff nailing a challenge to the door of the Notre Dame Athletic Department. The game was a revival of the religious wars, as far as McGough was concerned.

Schwartz looked up. Pickle was eyeing him thoughtfully.

"Give me a one- or two-sentence description of Reformation Day," Pickle said.

"You mean, what it commemorates."

Pickle nodded as if to do more would convict him of ignorance. Schwartz took more than two sentences to describe Martin Luther's dramatic posting of the ninety-five theses on the door of the Wittenberg Cathedral.

"He nailed them to the door?"

"It was not an uncommon theological practice."

"You're kidding."

The assistant provost was a microbiologist for whom most of what went on on campus was incomprehensible. The fact that he had looked favorably on the proposal for an academic conference was an ambiguous endorsement. But then he had covered his bet by insisting that Roger Knight take part. The result was that Knight would give a major paper on the religious odyssey of Orestes Brownson, and Ronald Arbuthnot of Baylor would respond. Even that relatively simple project had been all but crippled by the redoubtable Hazel Nootin. Now she had gone to her reward, and, in the words of Pickle, it was a whole new ball game.

"Did you know we have a Baylor alumnus on our faculty?" It was this rabbit for which Pickle had apparently called the meeting to pull out of his hat.

"No I didn't."

"He teaches philosophy." Pickle seemed about to add something, then thought it prudent not to. Philosophy was an enigma to the microbiologist. He had been told that semesters were spent asking whether the soul was a computer, whether you could know what someone else was thinking, whether genocide was wrong. They just talked—Pickle couldn't believe it. But he dragged his mind back to the point of the meeting. "Dave Solomon. I asked him to come." He looked at his watch. "He's late."

There was a flurry in the outer office, a high-pitched voice making excuses to Pickle's secretary, and then a burly man, his coat open to reveal a rotund torso, hair swept forward Caesar-like, and with eyebrows that seemed to have a mind of their own, entered, came to a stop, and smiled vaguely in various directions. This was Dave Solomon, Notre Dame professor of philosophy, alumnus of Baylor.

"I thought Dave could do liaison," Pickle said.

"Hey, I'm a married man."

"This is Austin Schwartz," Pickle introduced.

"Your son plays soccer."

"You're taking violin lessons."

"Piano. I want to play Bach with pleasure before I die."

The two men shook hands. Solomon was taking sporadic music lessons from the woman who taught Schwartz's son violin, and Solomon's daughter was the assistant coach of the same son's soccer team. Thus in the little world of Notre Dame do independent lines of causality meet and overlap and suggest that nothing is an accident.

"Tell us about Baylor," Pickle said, settling behind his desk.

Schwartz tuned out the paean of praise that followed. The elation he had felt at the removal of the main obstacle to a smooth conference altered. Not to be burdened with the conference at all was momentarily attractive. After all, it was no longer what he had envisaged. His notion had been a scholarly effort to show that the great divisions of the sixteenth century had been mountains made out of molehills. *Sola fides?* In a sense, why not? He knew all kinds of Catholic theologians who thought they could go a long way toward accommodating the phrase Luther had fashioned by altering the Bible. Whether or not there would be movement in the opposite direction toward the acceptance of merit was more chancy. In a lull in Solomon's tribute to his alma mater, Schwartz asked him what he thought of it.

"Merit? I don't know. Are you serious about *sola fides?*" Solomon wore the expression that had become familiar to Schwartz over the years as he engaged in ecumenical dialogue. It meant that Solomon smelled a compromise that went too far.

"There was a statement in *First Things* signed by both Protestant and Catholic theologians."

"Agreeing on merit?"

"The emphasis was on *sola fides.*"

Pickle was clearly impatient with the discussion. He had suffered Solomon's pitch for Baylor without demur, but he was damned if he was going to permit a theological discussion to go on in the privacy of his own office.

"Save all that for the big day," he advised.

"Why don't you talk with Roger Knight?" Solomon suggested.

Roger Knight. The suggestion reignited Schwartz's resentment. He was getting sick and tired of being referred to Roger Knight every time he turned around.

"Good idea," Pickle cried, springing from his chair. "I want to thank both of you for dropping by."

At the door, he detained Solomon. As he went on through the outer office, Schwartz heard Pickle ask Solomon if he would sit with the presidents of Notre Dame and Baylor during the game.

"Wow," said Solomon. "Great."

"Bring your wife," Pickle added.

Schwartz went off down the hall feeling more than ever like a fifth wheel.

21

PHIL ATTENDED THE WAKE FOR Hazel Nootin in company with Waring. Roger would go to the funeral Mass the following morning. The wake was a sad occasion. For all the publicity her violent death had attracted, there was a small turnout at the funeral home. Alfred, the bearded son by Fig's first wife, was there in support of his father. His other son, Bernie, was with the Seventh Fleet but supposedly on his way home as well. As if the enormity of what had happened had just now struck him, Fig Nootin stood in the doorway of the showing room, arms limp at his sides, mouth open, staring around. Alfred draped an arm across his father's shoulders and tried to lead him to a couch. Fig shook his head.

"It's all my fault."

Philip could sense Waring stirring beside him. Would there be a great revelation, an admission of guilt? Waring was a phlegmatic man, but he had said over dinner that the funeral of the victim was often the most important step in an investigation.

"Sit down, Dad," Alfred urged. His voice was that of a son, but in size and strength he overshadowed his father. He glared at Waring as if telling him to pay no attention to what his father said.

"I let her down," Fig said bleakly.

"We all did, Dad."

"No. You boys were like sons to her."

Alfred's grip tightened and he half forced his father to a couch, where they sat and Fig burst into tears. Alfred sat beside him chewing his lip. The grief of the principals affected the vis-

123

itors, and all eyes were damp when Father Carmody arrived to lead the rosary.

Philip went to a chair in the hallway outside and pondered the investigation of the death of Hazel Nootin. Waring seemed no nearer to knowing who was responsible for the death of the woman than Philip himself. As far as he knew, Waring knew nothing that he did not. What did they know?

- On Tuesday night, Hazel Nootin was apparently followed across the parking lot of the University Club, assaulted on the lawn between the lot and the street, strangled with her own scarf.

- The body had been discovered by a campus security patrol some hours after death had occurred.

- Some hours before Hazel's death, her husband had punched out Watts when he made an insulting remark about Hazel.

- Watts had been irked by the arbitrary and insulting manner in which Hazel dealt with him and others.

- Watts had gone on from the club to a lecture in the Knights of Columbus Hall given by Roger Knight.

- Fig Nootin had apparently stayed in the club bar until after midnight, according to Earl the bartender. "He closed the place."

- Austin Schwartz was preparing the conference about which Watts had crossed swords with Hazel and eventually with Fig Newton.

There seemed to be at least three possible authors of the violent death of Hazel Nootin, none of whom seemed completely promising:

(1) An irate Watts had motivation from his combined anger at Hazel and Fig.

(2) Fig himself could have killed his wife. Neither Earl nor anyone else could say that he had not left the club in the course of the night. "He went to the john," Earl had said. "Regularly."

(3) Schwartz? This was the most remote possibility of all. Like Watts, Schwartz had attended Roger's lecture. There was no reason to think that he had been so enraged by Hazel's high-handed manner that he would have stalked and strangled her.

From the funeral home, Waring and Phil went on to the University Club to have a drink, perhaps to be stirred to insight by the scene of the crime. Philip went through the same thought process out loud.

Waring took a long pull at his drink and then shook his head. "None of them. Nootin isn't going to step outside, strangle his wife, and then return to his stool at the bar. The other two were at a lecture, a nice place to simmer down and forget what a pain in the neck Hazel Nootin could be."

This description went uncontested by those with whom she worked. Indeed, within the convention of speaking well of the dead, they more than supported it. She had never accepted the notion that program directors were in the business of facilitating programs. For Hazel, the client was the enemy of her peace and quiet, come to disturb her day and aggravate her with a hundred silly requests. She had become master of the delayed insult. It was her special delight to enlist the client's laughter at the clownish behavior of one who, it dawned on the client, was himself. No one seemed to think it unlikely that someone would have wanted to strangle Hazel Nootin.

"Could it have been someone she worked with?" Phil said.

"Not unless they can bilocate. They were all elsewhere at the time of death," Waring confirmed.

"Hmmm."

"Maybe it was a bearded stranger."

"He operates out of Cleveland," Phil said.

Waring looked at him quizzically.

"A joke," Phil said. "Never mind."

22

FOR THE SUBJECT OF THE PAPER he would present at Austin Schwartz's conference, Roger Knight had finally chosen the episode in Orestes Brownson's life when he had come under the suspicion of heterodoxy. The key text was an essay Brownson published in October 1861 on "Reading and Study of the Scriptures." In it he linked a loss of piety with failure to read the Bible and suggested a kind of historical declension from reading the Scriptures straight.

The fathers of the Church pored over the Scriptures and expounded them. The medieval doctors studied and epitomized the fathers but were at one remove from Scripture itself. Then came the theologians, whose compendia represented a further decline, until we come to modern professors, who have fallen as low as one can without becoming nothing at all. The same downward tendency can be descried in devotional and ascetic literature.

This had brought the accusation that Brownson despised Anselm and Bonaventure and Thomas Aquinas. Untrue, no doubt, but he certainly ranked them far below the fathers. Roger had some critical things to say about Brownson's generalities regarding the medieval masters, wondering how familiar with their works he really was. But the point of the paper was to compare Brownson's attitude toward Scripture favorably with subsequent encyclicals and directives of the Magisterium.

The paper was drafted and its point seemed interesting enough, but Roger began to wonder at its fittingness to playing the role in the conference it was destined to play. He outlined another paper about Brownson's old opponent in *The Dublin Review*, W. G. Ward. Ward led on to Newman, and then Roger had it. He would speak on Brownson's criticism of Newman's "Development of Christian Doctrine." Here was something controversial enough for the conference. Perhaps the men from Baylor would find Brownson a congenial figure on this topic.

Then Phil came home from the wake and put on a pan of milk for their nightcap of cocoa.

"How was it?"

"Nootin is beginning to crumble."

"How's the investigation going?"

Phil's report was not encouraging. Waring's supposition that the murderer might not be connected with Hazel at all, that it had been just a stranger who for whatever irrational reason decided to assault and strangle her, was indeed discouraging.

"But it's highly unlikely any of the three did it."

"Then there must be a fourth."

"A bearded stranger."

Roger shook his head. "No, it couldn't have been a stranger."

"Why not?"

"Because she wasn't alarmed."

"How do you know that?"

"From what you've told me."

Roger reviewed the meager facts Phil had passed on to him. It would have been difficult to justify the supposition that Hazel had been stalked or even followed on the basis of those facts.

"He probably was walking at her side."

"He?"

"The man with the size-sixteen shoes."

The police lab had collected every impression imaginable from the surface of the parking lot, covering a ten-yard swath from the entrance to the club to where the body was found. There were tire tracks, footprints, dozens of indecipherable marks, all of them being dutifully cataloged and described. Roger had plucked from the printout of the items the marks made by a very large pair of feet wearing shoes whose crepe bottoms had made a venetian blind–like impression on the dusty tarmac. Doubtless it was the weight of the man that accounted for the relative clarity of the impression.

"There is no way to establish with accuracy how long ago any of those prints might have been made, Roger."

"Except Hazel Nootin's."

"That's different. We have independent criteria."

"But that gives you a point of comparison for the others."

"Do you want a Cinderella investigation—a search for a man with big feet?"

"Large soles," Roger mused. And then he smiled. "Magnanimous."

There was a time to reply to Roger and a time to remain silent. Phil remained silent.

Roger too fell silent. His mind was tugged back toward the attractive topic of Orestes Brownson and the paper he must have ready within a few days. A copy must be sent to his commentator in Waco, Ronald Arbuthnot. But there were the fitful reports of the investigation into the death of Hazel Nootin that Phil brought home to tease his mind away from nineteenth-century disputes and the ancient lore of Notre Dame.

Perhaps someday a book on strange campus deaths would be written. It could include events from the worker who had plunged from the tower of the library while it was being built, to the cleaning woman who had been found murdered in the old AeroSpace Building one morning. And once a tramp had wedged himself into a tight, warm place in the main building and had been unable to get out. He was found dead after who knew what agonies. And, going all the way back to the chronicles Father Sorin had kept of the first ten or fifteen years of the university, there had been drownings in the lake and various illnesses that cut scythe-like through the little community.

The death of Hazel Nootin must be added to that macabre list now. But it must not go down unsolved. That mysterious deaths a century before, even a decade before, went unexplained was one thing. But it seemed intolerable that in this day and age a living human person could be attacked and killed on campus and the killer walk off unknown and unpunished.

What Roger had come to know of Fig Nootin while the man was in the house installing the magnificent cabinetwork and walls of bookshelves was inconclusive. It was Roger's belief, solidly grounded in the doctrine of Original Sin, that anyone might, under appropriate circumstances and after earlier un-dramatic betrayals, commit any crime, no matter how heinous. As a bachelor and the brother of a bachelor, Roger found the re-lationships between husbands and wives unintelligible. First of all, there was the undeniable fact that a man and woman who seemed at opposite poles in everything should be romantically inclined. Second was the coexistence of love and, well, hate would be too strong, but nonlove in the same couple, also fre-quently a fact and yet unintelligible.

One of the items in Fig's standard repertoire while he worked—he seemed to think that it was part of the contract that he must entertain the one who had hired him with anecdotes and a ceaseless flow of words—was the wife he called Haze. Haze and Fig. Roger shook his head. Those nicknames might have summed up the matrimonial mystery. There was never a note of bitterness in Fig's voice when he spoke of his wife. He seemed amused by her eccentricities. He was certainly aware of them, since he invoked them to explain why his sons had never be-come close to his second wife, but he himself seemed more en-amored of her faults than angered by them. That he had come to her defense in the bar of the club was perfectly consistent with the Fig Nootin Roger had come reluctantly to know.

Austin Schwartz? An enigmatic figure, one of the almost anonymous members of the faculty, lost in the shuffle and not minding it much. He was neither a great teacher nor a poor one, neither a productive scholar nor one without at least a few achievements. His master's thesis on Scotus's notion of *haecceitas* showed up regularly in bibliographies, but his far more ambitious doctoral dissertation on Scotus and Heidegger, although it had been published by an obscure house, had fallen into deep and, Roger thought, deserved oblivion. Of late, Schwartz's research wandered through the thicket of nominalism and the Reformation. It was out of that latter-day interest that the idea of the conference must have sprung.

"And to counter the notion," Schwartz told Roger over lunch," that the faculty is simply a tutorial force employed to ensure the eligibility of athletes."

"No one thinks that, Austin."

"I could name names."

Roger had waited, but Austin did not name names. He said, "I would like to eclipse football."

"You sound like the Reverend Edwina Marciniak."

"The little woman who was at your lecture."

"Formidable," Roger said.

"Does she have any academic credentials?"

"I don't know."

"It occurred to me that she might want to come to our conference," Schwartz said.

"I have a feeling she will be there."

"Then I might just as well invite her."

"Wonderful."

Roger found it impossible to imagine Austin Schwartz as the murderer of Hazel Nootin. Schwartz had mentioned his struggles with Hazel.

"Mano a mano, Roger. She has a black belt in bureaucratic rough-and-tumble."

"I suppose people over there find the faculty hard to deal with," Roger observed.

Schwartz did not find the suggestion plausible. For him, the faculty was the university. Everyone else, trustee, administrator, business office, foundation, staff, maintenance, ground crew, hall rectors, students, had such significance as they had because of their more or less close relationship to the faculty.

"The analogy of academe," Roger called it when he described this outlook for Philip.

He knew too of the attitude of librarians and archivists toward those faculty members who treated them as if they were invisible or stupid, and this despite the fact that a little inquiry would have revealed that these men and women were in many cases as highly educated as the teaching faculty.

Of course Roger had no desire to be a traitor to his class. The treason of clerks was aimed first at themselves. Professors must hang together if not at all costs, then at least in the short run.

Watts. Roger found the public relations man the most intriguing of the three unlikely suspects Phil had identified. If Roger could, at least on theological grounds, see Fig murdering his wife or Schwartz coming down upon her like a wolf on the fold, his cohorts all gleaming in purple and gold or however the poem went, it cost him almost no imaginative effort to put Watts in the role of stealthy strangler.

Philip himself could see that what might fancifully be called the alibis of Nootin and Schwartz did not preclude their being at the place of murder at the appropriate time. In the case of Watts, this was far more plausibly the case. Watts himself was unsure of time and places during the fateful night.

"He's an alcoholic," Fenwick had said emphatically when Roger ran into Watts's boss in the huddle. He was half hiding in a corner eating a pizza. He had said, half belligerently, half sheepishly, that he was on a diet.

"Is that the low-cal pizza?"

"Do they have them?"

"Not during the week."

Obviously Fenwick was a literal man. Or simply a guilty eater who would like to turn his vice into a virtue.

"Do you mean he has stopped drinking?"

"Oh, regularly. But he can't keep away from it."

"Poor man."

"If he weren't the best writer I have, I would fire him." He paused. "Not that firing anyone is easily done. It may not even be possible. Have you had anything to do with Human Resources?"

"It sounds like a biology lab doing illicit research."

"Watts thinks the people in the CCE are bad. He should deal with the monsters in Human Resources."

"If they provide him job security, he might like them. He's talked to you about the CCE?"

"Talked to me! It's an obsession. I half expect him to dance on the grave of that woman, what's-her-name."

What's-her-name. *Sic transit gloria mundi.* "Hazel Nootin," Roger said.

"Did Watts show you his doll?"

"Doll?"

"The one he sticks pins in. His Hazel doll."

Long-distance violence could have been transmuted into something up close and personal.

"Do you drink?" Watts had asked when Roger met with him again about the unsatisfactory interview Watts had conducted in Roger's office the day after the body of Hazel was discovered.

"No."

"Not at all or not much?"

"Not at all. I studied the biology of the effects alcohol has on the nervous system and lost any interest I might have had in drinking."

"I know what it does," Watts said with a grim smile. "Have you ever had the experience of not being able to account for whole stretches of time when you were up and moving around?"

"Sometimes I can't remember getting to where I am."

"This is like that. Only worse. When your brother asked me about the night Hazel Nootin got it? The truth is I can't account for some of it."

An action a human being does not know he is performing is not a human action. Was it disrespectful to hope that whoever had killed Hazel Nootin had known what he was doing and had done it deliberately? Anything else would seem to reduce her to the status of What's-her-name.

Tomorrow he would attend her funeral.

23 ➤ bells of Sacred Heart Basilica went unnoticed by students hurrying back and forth to classes, or, if noticed, its significance was not grasped. What do the young have to do with death and mourning and the burial of the dead?

In her room, Agatha paused and listened to the bells. Did they ring every day like that? It was hard to believe she had never noticed them before. She decided that they were something special. What did they mean? She did not connect the bells with the death of the program director from the CCE.

The murder had been covered in *The Observer,* but it might have taken place on the moon. Didn't they have anyone who could draw a map of the area, put an X where the body was—make a bit of a fuss over it?

"You must all be terrified," Edwina said, calling again to see if Agatha had been strangled yet.

Her funeral, Agatha thought. That's what the bells are for.

She had a quick breakfast in the south dining hall, and when she came out, stood listening, but the sound of the bells had stopped. Agatha drifted across the mall, between the bookstore and the Knights of Columbus Hall, and along the street that ran behind Walsh and Sorin. Corby Hall, where most of the priests lived, seemed yellow behind a black lattice of trees. In front was the statue of Father Corby blessing the Union troops before the Battle of Gettysburg. He wore a frock coat and his right hand was raised. Fair Catch Corby, he was called. On the road in the front of the church a hearse was parked and behind it several somber vehicles and then a row of cars that seemed to have arrived together.

A man wearing a gray overcoat with a black velvet collar was smoking a cigarette beside the hearse.

"Whose funeral is it?" Agatha asked him.

He looked momentarily alarmed. "The woman who worked here." Then he had it. "Mrs. Nootin."

"The one who was killed?"

"Are you a student here?"

"Yes. Can I go in?"

He hurried up the steps and pulled open the door for her. Agatha thanked him, slipping by his tobaccoy breath and inside. The door closed behind her. The door between the vestibule and the church was closed. Racks on the walls were full of pamphlets. Blessed Brother Andre, the Canadian CSC brother they hoped would be canonized someday. There was a little table, too. There was a kind of security in the church now and someone usually sat at the table, on duty, monitoring visitors, welcoming guests, making sure everyone knew this was the house of God.

The outside door opened and Edwina pushed past the man in the gray coat. She saw Agatha immediately.

"Are you waiting for me?"

"I didn't know you were coming."

"Of course you did. I told you. Come on."

Out of habit, Agatha dipped her fingers into the holy water font and extended them to Edwina. She scowled at the wet fingertips and then at Agatha. Agatha made the sign of the cross with great deliberation.

There were perhaps a dozen pews toward the front of the church that were more or less full. The casket, draped in white, stood in the middle aisle, pushed almost to the steps leading up to the sanctuary. The cousins stood for a moment in the back. The huge main altar, gold and busy with figures, stood behind the plain slab facing the people on which Mass was now offered.

Far in the back, under the illumined statue of Mary high in its niche, the Bernini altar was visible, white and gold, looking almost edible. Edwina looked sternly around. All of this would be familiar to her, but now she claimed to despise it all. Agatha took her cousin's hand and squeezed it. Her fingers were still damp with holy water. She might have been driving out devils.

A nervous, frowning man who might have been the twin of the one outside sneaking a smoke glided toward them.

"Come, be seated," he said, and took Agatha's arm. She half expected him to ask "Bride or groom?"

But then she was being taken up the aisle on the arm of the man. Edwina was audible behind her. By the time they came to a stop, Agatha was glad to duck into the pew. Edwina came bowling in after her. Some heads had turned to see who the delinquents were.

The priest was circling the altar, swinging a censer, causing great clouds of sweet-smelling smoke to rise. He seemed to want to envelop the altar with clouds of incense. Then he came down the steps and circled the coffin, incensing as he went.

"What on earth?" Edwina said in a stage whisper.

"I've never been to a funeral before," Agatha said in a real whisper.

"This is a pagan rite."

Heads turned again and Edwina stared at the starers. For a moment, Agatha feared that Edwina would disrupt the ceremony. But she subsided and then the sound of a sob came to them from a front pew. A middle-aged man stood between two young men who were trying to console him. Agatha remembered that someone was dead and others were here to mourn her. She felt awful just coming in like this out of curiosity. One of the mourners was the great fat Roger Knight. He wore a sad expression but his eyes darted about as he came down the aisle after the service. He recognized Edwina and held out a hand. She took it for a moment and then he was gone.

"Why did you come?" she asked Edwina when it was over.

They were still in their pew, having watched the casket being wheeled out, followed by the weeping man supported by the two young men.

"To remind myself how bad this is."

"Did you know the woman who was killed?"

"No."

Edwina took Agatha's elbow and eased her into the main aisle, and they walked to the entrance. There was still congestion outside. The casket had been wheeled into the hearse and the man with the gray topcoat and black velvet collar was behind the wheel.

"Those are his sons," Edwina said, indicating the two young men who were helping the still sobbing man into the backseat of a long black car. That must be Nootin, the husband of the woman who had been killed, Agatha thought.

"They're taking it better than their father," she observed.

"She wasn't their mother."

"How do you know these things?" Agatha asked.

"Don't you read the paper?"

Edwina always seemed to be scolding her about something. "I have to get to class."

"Why did you come to this funeral?" Edwina asked.

"I was in the neighborhood."

24　ＥＤＷＩＮＡ　ＷＡＴＣＨＥＤ　ＨＥＲ　ＳＡＳＳＹ cousin walk away. Then Agatha turned and waved. Edwina wanted to call her back; she wanted to talk to somebody, to make more real what she knew by expressing it in words, although she knew she should not do that. It was not the professional way to behave. A confidence was a confidence. But such a coup! It seemed unfair that such a triumph should be hers yet she could reveal it to no one. Of course she could have sworn Agatha to silence.

No, she was condemned to an anonymous victory and that was all there was to it. In the meantime she wandered along the road that dipped down to the lake. There were benches there and a population explosion of geese and ducks. Canadian geese. The immigration laws should apply to them, Edwina thought. They were a menace.

Edwina shooed several geese out of her path and sat upon a bench. On another occasion she might have reflected on the parallel between all those unwanted geese and the Catholic Church's plan to outnumber her enemies by urging unlimited procreation on her members. Edwina was not deceived by the effort to make it seem a moral issue. She understood a political move when she saw one, and this was raw power exerted on a global scale. If the plan worked, the only whites left would be Catholic and the rest would be blacks. What could stop them?

But the urgency of this problem faded at the memory of the visit to her office of Elijah Samuel Phipps.

"Yes?" she had yelped when the huge black male filled up

the door of her office. At first she did not recognize him and, when she did recall her less than glorious encounter with the boy at Hope Baptist, she prepared for battle. This man had laughed when she was introduced to him as a lady preacher.

"I'm a Baptist."

"This is the Independent Protestant Church of Jesus Christ and His Almighty Parent."

"Protestant?"

"Yes."

He had squeezed into the office, looked at the dimensions of the chair Edwina gestured toward, and remained standing.

"Preacher Stone doesn't understand."

Was this about some intramural quarrel among Baptists? Edwina had no wish to fan the flames of dissent in communions other than the Roman Catholic.

"He's a Notre Dame fan. He wants them to win."

Dear God, sports. "Why have you come to me?"

"Something Preacher Stone said."

"And what was that?"

"He said, 'That lady preacher would agree with you.' "

"Tell me about it."

He was a remarkably articulate young man. For purposes of comfort, Edwina had taken him into the church, where a pew was wide enough to accommodate him. Elijah faced a crisis of conscience and had received no help from Stone—unless one counted what had doubtless been meant as a demeaning remark about Edwina as help. In any case it had brought him here.

"Baylor is a Baptist university. It's where I should be playing."

"Why do you say that?"

"I'm a Texan and a Baptist, and they offered me a scholarship but instead I came to Notre Dame. I didn't know we would ever play Baylor. There has never been a game between Baylor and Notre Dame before. I can't help Notre Dame beat Baylor."

"You mean you can't help a Catholic school beat a Protestant school?"

"A Baptist school!"

Delicacy was imperative, Edwina realized, so she had stifled her impulse to launch a tirade on the Catholic Church in general and the University of Notre Dame in particular. But she took her cue from the softspoken young man, who was more sorrowful than angry.

"Does Notre Dame need you?"

He had looked at her, surprised. "I'm the quarterback."

It all came back to her now, the mountains of sports trivia she had tried to rinse from her mind with biblical lore. Suddenly she could have rattled off the names of every Notre Dame quarterback since Rockne himself. And this young man was the latest in that long, distinguished line. Edwina felt a moment of awe. And then the enormity of what he was saying struck her. Elijah was the Notre Dame quarterback. Doubtless he was an essential key to Notre Dame.

"You've been going to practice?"

"I never miss practice."

"Of course in practice you don't have to play against Baylor."

"I don't know what to do."

Edwina had let the silence swell and then said, "I think you do."

He looked at her with large, sad eyes. An eternity ticked by. Then his eyes dropped and he nodded his head.

"You could be sick," she had suggested.

"I'm never sick."

She was on the verge of telling him he must hide. If they began to exert pressure on him, they could easily turn his mind away from his doubts. Before he knew what was happening, he could be in uniform and on the field and facing Baylor. Edwina thought about that. Should she suggest he play in the expectation that his divided mind would prevent him from playing well?

She realized that what she wanted was a Baylor victory over Notre Dame. Her opposition to the game had been on the assumption that Baylor would lose. Not only would they come willingly into the enemy's camp, they would suffer a humiliating defeat there. But what if they won!

Somehow she was certain that Elijah would play his heart out if he went onto that field. He might lament beforehand that he must defeat Baylor and he could feel remorse afterward, but no trained athlete could fail to play to the peak of his abilities once the contest was engaged.

"You must lead yourself out of temptation," Edwina had said.

He looked at her.

"You must deliver yourself from evil."

Once more she had waited, wondering if she had gone too far. These were deep waters and he was a giant fish, but she must yield and reel him in with dexterity and art if she were to land the catch of her career.

"How?"

"You can't pretend to be sick."

"No."

"You can't go on the field and not play well."

"No."

"You can't stay on campus or they will come and sweet-talk you into playing that game."

He nodded. And then he said, "I'll leave town."

The fish was landed. She said no more. She had actually embraced him before he left and then turned in her empty church and faced the far end, where her pulpit loomed. For a moment she'd wished there were an altar there, a tabernacle, a small red lamp gleaming in the gloom. She wanted to kneel and thank God for delivering her enemies into her hands.

An hour later she was wondering if Elijah would retain the courage of his convictions. She had gone to the campus and attended the funeral of Hazel Nootin in the mad hope that she might see Elijah and at least give him a sign of encouragement if she could not talk with him. Now, sitting by the lake, ignoring the importunate geese, her feeling of triumph was eroded by the fear that Elijah would cave in.

25 ELIJAH SET HIS ALARM FOR four o'clock, but that was unnecessary. He did not sleep all night. In the Bible there were stories of men who had stayed awake the whole night through. There was the story of Jacob wrestling with the angel, there were numerous verses recounting sleepless nights, there was Samuel, who had been called from sleep. But there were also the disciples who had fallen asleep in the Garden of Olives. Elijah had always had the sad certainty that if he had been there he would have done the same.

It was easy to think that you would have been different if you had been Peter and the servant girl asked if you were not a follower of Jesus. As a boy, Elijah had imagined himself shouting a defiant "Yes!" He would be led away into the prison where they were keeping Jesus and he wouldn't care what they did to him; he would be loyal.

Now he faced a real test, the greatest test he had ever faced. He lay sleepless in his bed as the digital clock passed twelve and then began to move in little lurches through the early hours of morning. Saturday would be game day. He felt the thrill of excitement, of course, but he was sure now that he would do what he had to do.

That little lady preacher was funny and she wasn't a Baptist, but he was glad he had gone to see her. She was a fighter, he could see that. And she understood that some things could not be compromised. Pastor Stone was as big a fan as any Irishman from Chicago. As far as Notre Dame went, he was an honorary

Catholic, Catholic for a day. He actually wanted Baylor to be defeated by Notre Dame.

But Reverend Edwina understood the problem. She had provided him with strength when he needed it. Once or twice he had wanted to go back and be reenforced by her unwavering dedication to principle. He had told no one what he was going to do. The previous evening he had made a long-distance phone call to Bristlo and talked to his father briefly and then at great length to his mother.

"You reading your Bible, son?"

"Every day."

"You do that."

"Yes, Ma."

In the background his father shouted "Go Irish!" Even so, Elijah was sure his father would understand what he was going to do. Or his mother would, and she could explain it to his father. A man could not accept a call as a Baptist preacher if he had contributed to the humiliation of Baylor University. Maybe Pastor Stone thought you could do that, but Elijah had been raised differently. The Reverend Edwina's steely encouragement had given him the support he needed. He was resolved to use subterfuge or whatever biblical trick he could think of to deceive his teammates and the coaching staff and to be out of reach and out of call when Saturday arrived.

Thus it was that, early on the Tuesday morning, he rose before five, dressed hurriedly, and then took the overnight bag he had packed before going to bed and crept out of the dormitory. Already there was a student or two out for his or her morning run, puffing through the misty morning toward some ideal of health or beauty that was, alas, destined to exist only in the mind's eye.

Elijah crossed the mall and passed the south dining hall, not yet open but already wafting its delectable odors on the morning air. For a moment the prospect of an ordinary day—breakfast, class, practice—exercised an enormous attraction, but then the stern voice of Reverend Edwina spoke in memory more imperious than the voice of conscience, and he continued southward, behind O'Neill Hall, heading for the boarding stop of the bus that was grandly titled the United Limo.

This was a cheap way to get to Michiana Regional Airport—Hoosier International, to the irreverent—and beyond. The bus pushed on to Portage, to Michigan City, to a transfer point to Midway, and on to O'Hare. It had been some time since Elijah had ridden the limo, since most of his traveling now was with the team and they flew in the university's aircraft. But he had got hold of a schedule and would board the first bus of the morning when it arrived from Mishawaka.

He was now traversing what had once been the back nine of the golf course. He had listened to Father Riehle recount triumphs on the old course, not to be compared with the new links north of the campus, but then the new course was not yet heavy with memories. It was difficult for Elijah to grasp the sense of sacrilege Riehle felt, that a historic golf course had been summarily turned into a building site for the four new dorms that now looked across the road toward the back of the dining hall. Beyond them now was the new bookstore and, on Notre Dame Avenue, the alumni center. And there, beyond the guard shack, was the boundary fence of Cedar Grove Cemetery and, to the left of the campus entrance, the shelter where one waited for the limo.

As he approached the shelter, Elijah saw that someone was already waiting there. He stopped. The whole point of leaving this early was to avoid any possibility of being observed. If another student saw him board the bus, he would be recognized and his flight would be known. Worse, they would know where to look for him.

As he stood there indecisively, he heard a piercing whistle. It came from the shelter. The person standing there was gesturing at him. And then he saw that it was Reverend Edwina. He hurried toward her. She thrust out her hand when he came into the shelter and pumped his arm vigorously.

"Good man," she said.

Elijah nodded. He was glad she was here. The better he got to know her, the more like a Baptist she seemed. The way a Baptist ought to be, he added to himself, thinking of the waffling Pastor Stone. Perhaps he should speak to her of switching allegiances. But then she could not be a preacher if she became a Baptist.

"Have you had breakfast?"

"No."

"Here." She thrust a plastic lunch bucket into his hand. She must have had it concealed behind her. "When you get to O'Hare, the Hilton will be just across the street from where the limo stops. There is a room reserved for you there."

"Under Phipps?"

"Hardly. Marciniak."

"How do you spell that?"

She dug a card from her pocket and gave it to him. "Pronounce it."

"Mar-chin—"

She stopped him. "The *c* is soft. As in 'sin.' " She then rehearsed him on the name. It was a way of passing the time. But then she cried, "There it is!"

A large red hulk of a bus had turned onto Notre Dame Avenue and was approaching. It passed the entrance to another service road some yards farther on and then made a great loop before coming to a stop at the shelter. There was a creaking of brakes and then a hissing of compressed air as the door opened. A merry little man with a potbelly bounced down the steps, almost bumping into Edwina.

"Go on in, Andrew," she said, nudging Elijah in the ribs. "Give me your ticket."

As he boarded the bus he could hear her babbling away with the driver. She turned over his ticket and then got on the bus herself to give him the yellow receipt. "Sit way in back," she urged. "This guy loves to talk."

148

She made a movement with her hand, Elijah ducked down, and she gave him a kiss on the cheek. "God go with you."

It was a dramatic moment. He had closed his eyes when he dipped down to her and her lips on his cheek might have been his mother's. Elijah went down the aisle to the back of the bus and wedged himself into a seat. His eyes were clouded with tears. Edwina had gotten off the bus, the door was closed, and the vehicle began to move forward.

Elijah pressed his face against the window and got a glimpse of the golden dome, and then the stadium rose on the horizon, blotting out the sun that was still low in the east, and Elijah realized the seriousness of what he was doing. He was fleeing the campus, deserting his teammates, letting down the coaches. The student body was a vaguer constituency. He pressed his forehead against the cold surface of the window and repeated to himself that what he was doing was right. The only right thing. A Baptist could do no other.

26　　　　THE BAYLOR DELEGATION AR-
rived on Tuesday night and was met by a
fleet of cars driven by graduate students. Eventually they would
be distributed in various homes, but the first order of business
was dinner at the Morris Inn. There were early guests already arrived for the game but for all that the inn was not crowded, and
Austin Schwartz could half believe that he had been misin
formed by the late Hazel Nootin when she'd told him there
wasn't a hope in hell that he could lodge his participants there.

"You'd be lucky to find rooms for them as close as Michigan
City," she'd harped.

The Baylor delegation, the soul of politeness, expressed
their delight that they would be housed in faculty residences
rather than on campus. Ronald Arbuthnot, their spokesman,
made a little speech expressing their collective hope that the
conference would fulfill its purpose and that all of them would
come away from it better than they had gone into it.

Schwartz responded, lifting his water glass in a toast. Some
of the Baylor people had ordered beer and, thus encouraged,
their hosts had ordered their favorite drinks. Still, making the
toast with water seemed appropriate.

"Not because you are Baptists," Schwartz said, and paused
for the laughter that did not come. "But because you have come
to Notre Dame du Lac. Our Lady of the Lake. This is not, however, lake water. For all that, welcome and may we have a productive conference."

Old friends talked academic shop for the rest of the meal

and into the evening. Roger Knight, presiding at one of the round tables in the dining room, told anecdotes about his brother's life as a private investigator. That led on to talk of the recent tragedy on campus, the murder of Hazel Nootin.

"Perhaps it was a disgruntled student."

"Oh, she wasn't on the faculty."

Professorial paranoia was next revealed as one person after another told of how he or she thought a determined vindictive student could wipe out half the faculty of Notre Dame in one fell blow.

"The ventilating system in Decio is an open invitation for a lethal gas."

"In or out?"

"Ho ho."

Stories of threats from students, usually empty, were exchanged. As the evening progressed, the group sounded more and more like habitués of the American Legion exchanging dubious war stories.

Philip came by after nine to pick up Roger and his guest, Stephen Tetzel. Roger knew Tetzel's work on biblical criticism but had never before met him.

"Any relation?"

"To whom?"

"Wasn't Tetzel one of the preachers Luther accused of selling indulgences?" Roger asked.

"Good Lord. I hope you won't bring that up tomorrow."

"Not if you don't bring up indulgences."

"On Reformation Day?"

"I don't know what you two are talking about," Phil said. "Have you heard the news?"

"What news?"

"One of the players is missing."

"Who?"

"ESP."

"The quarterback!"

"You talking about Phipps?" Tetzel said. "It was a dark day in Waco when he turned down the offer of a fellowship."

They talked about what a lacuna there would be in the Irish game plan if ESP really was missing. But of course none of them really thought he was. There had to be some explanation, Roger assured Tetzel, not wanting to alert the Baylor contingent. Philip became grave.

"What is it, Phil?"

"Nothing."

Clearly it was the kind of nothing that was something. Roger waited until they were home and Tetzel was settled in his room. Phil was in the den watching television. He looked up after Roger had stood beside his chair for several minutes.

"Waring thinks he knows why ESP can't be found."

"Oh?"

"Remember that size-sixteen shoe print they found in the University Club parking lot?"

Called in by a frantic coaching staff, Phil had gone to Phipps's residence hall. He had had Waring in tow, and it was the South Bend detective who had picked up a shoe in Phipps's closet and turned it over.

"The sole was the kind that would make the sort of print found in the parking lot. And it was a big shoe. Waring took it with him."

"Have you talked with him since?"

"It's a match."

There were not many things that could keep Roger Knight from a good night's sleep, but what Phil had said about Elijah Samuel Phipps made him feel as if he had drunk a full six-pack of Mello Yello, the soft drink that is carbonated caffeine. He lay on his back staring at an ectoplasmic light that moved about on his ceiling. It was the reflection off the surface of his bedside glass of water of the night-light in the hallway. His restless movements sufficed to create a minor tide in the water of the glass, and that caused the ceiling reflection to seem almost animate above him.

For Elijah to be missing from the Notre Dame lineup on Saturday would be an athletic tragedy. But for him to come under suspicion in the strangling death of Hazel Nootin was a tragedy of a far more serious kind.

"Did he even know the woman?" Roger had wondered, talking with Phil over dinner that night.

"There's no reason to think so," Phil had answered.

"Is there any reason to think that he was near the University Club that night?"

Phil looked abject. He nodded. "He stopped by to talk to Earl after a late workout in Loftus. Earl is a Texan and they had that in common."

"He didn't serve him a drink, did he?"

"Oh no. ESP doesn't take a drop, according to Earl."

"So Waring asked him that."

"Wouldn't you?"

"How did he leave the club?" Roger asked.

"By the front door."

"So he would have walked across the lot on his way to his dorm."

"On almost the same line taken by Hazel Nootin," Phil observed.

"Who saw him last?"

"We'll start that kind of questioning in the morning. The coach is frantic."

"The Notre Dame coach?"

Weak humor. What would the Baylor coaching staff say when they heard that Notre Dame's key player seemed to be missing?

------▶

On the following morning, the participants in the academic conference gathered and Roger read his paper. He was still bothered by the news about Elijah when he began, but such are the marvels of the human mind that after a page or two he thought of nothing but what he was reading. Orestes Brownson had advanced as criticisms of the Catholic cult of the saints every caustic comment ever made by the most iconoclastic of Protestants. Then he had proceeded to answer them one by one.

"Brownson's attitude toward Mary undergoes an obvious change from the early days of his conversion. When Fathers Sorin and Hudson urged him to write for *Ave Maria,* a magazine whose chief purpose was to increase devotion to the mother of Jesus, Brownson's response was oblique. Sorin, who had an enthusiastic devotion to Mary, must have been disappointed by Brownson's first foray into Mariology."

"Did you say Mariolatry?" a female voice piped up.

"No, Edwina. You did."

"Sorry."

"There is no apology needed."

"I was apologizing for my hearing."

"Let he who has ears to hear . . ." Roger began.

"Let he or she . . ."

The Baylor contingent was surprised at the good grace with which Roger took this intervention by the pastor of the Independent Protestant Church of Jesus Christ and His Almighty Parent. He had introduced her from the podium before beginning his paper, identifying her as a local pastor with a more than passing interest in the Baylor–Notre Dame game.

"More than a punting interest, too," he'd remarked.

Edwina beamed at this attention. Indeed, throughout the morning her good cheer bordered on the manic. Meanwhile, Roger linked what he had said of Catholic devotion to the Blessed Virgin Mary with Newman's conception of the development of doctrine. During the coffee break, Edwina told Roger that he had made the best of a bad argument, adding, "I am dying to hear the rebuttal."

Rebuttal was too strong a word for Ronald Arbuthnot's response. Indeed, *response* was too strong a word for it. He took the occasion to speak on Paul as hero of the Baptist tradition. His use of the word *tradition* prompted Tetzel to deny there was any such thing as a Baptist tradition. What Arbuthnot emphasized was the common Baptist thinking that Paul of Tarsus was a heroic figure in the spread and defense of the teaching of Jesus. He then went through the scriptural passages Roger had stitched together in order to indicate the biblical basis of what Protestants, including Orestes Brownson before his conversion, thought was made up out of whole cloth.

The discussion was lively and roamed all over the universe of discourse. In the manner of academic discussions, any notion of there being sides fell away as each professor put forward his personal view of the matters under consideration. In the academy, Catholic or Protestant, private interpretation is the rule.

Edwina sat next to Roger at lunch. He had a great secret that he did not want to divulge to her, given her ambition to boycott Saturday's game. On her part, she seemed to be holding back too, but whatever it was, unlike Roger's secret, it was one that made it difficult for her not to wear a perpetual smile. This was such a change from her characteristic scowl that Roger commented on it.

"It is a treat for me to be able to kibitz on great minds at work," Edwina said.

"Did you lose your devotion to Mary when you lost your Catholic faith?"

"Devotion to Mary is a ploy to placate the oppressed women in the Church."

She went on, sounding a bit like Nietzsche. There was one morality for the masters and another for the slaves. Marian devotion was to keep the slaves content with their lot.

"What do you think of the Hail Mary pass?" Arbuthnot asked Edwina playfully.

"Does Baylor intend to throw one?" she wanted to know.

"We will fight valiantly; you can count on that."

"And lose?"

"We are not favored to win."

Edwina's smile was nearly out of control. And then it occurred to Roger that their secrets were the same and it was only their reactions that differed. The apparent disappearance of Elijah had given Edwina hope that a historic upset was in the making. He would have liked to quiz her on this point, but he did not want the Baylor delegation buzzing with gossip about Elijah.

In the afternoon, three local television stations came and took footage of the conference. Various participants were interviewed. An editor from *Notre Dame Magazine* talked with a Baylor man about the possibility of writing a piece on the Branch Davidian massacre.

"For the Notre Dame alumni magazine?"

"Oh, we're not an alumni magazine."

"I don't understand."

"We like to think of ourselves as an academic *Atlantic Monthly.*"

The Baylor professor edged away from his bearded interlocutor and looked around for help. Roger rescued him.

Pickle, the associate provost, represented the administration at the banquet that night. A nonalcoholic wine was served as well as the real article, but somewhere in the course of the evening the waitresses mixed up the bottles and the meal became festive. There was a general feeling that the beverage was better than ginger ale. When the mistake was discovered, there was much laughter.

"It's a miracle."

"Go fill some stone jars with water."

Ah, the innocent exchanges of the academic world. Austin Schwartz, who had drunk deeply from the right bottle, beamed at his colleagues and the guests from Baylor. He rose and began some impromptu remarks about Roger's paper, but Pickle pulled him down when his tongue became twisted. His effort to say that Roger had done his habitual best kept coming out profane.

In the van on the way home, Roger asked Phil anxiously, "Any word?"

"No."

There was no need to be more specific.

27 THERE WERE FOUR PEANUT
butter and jelly sandwiches in the lunch-
box Edwina had given him, as well as a plastic bottle of mineral
water. Elijah ate them all before the bus arrived at the South
Bend airport. Eating made him hungry and when the bus
stopped at LaPorte, he ran inside and bought several bags of regular M&M's. But he was ravenous again when the bus turned off
I-94 and headed into Michigan City.

The stop at Michigan City was at a Holiday Inn. With his bag
over his shoulder, Elijah got off before the new passengers
boarded. The driver had gone inside. In the lobby, Elijah stopped
and began to back toward the door through which he had entered: the lobby was filled with young men his age and of com-
parable size. It dawned on him that this was the Baylor football
team. This was where they would spend the nights prior to the
big game, bussing into South Bend to take their turn on the practice field. Or maybe, if they were shrewd, they had arranged to
use a local field, to stay out of range of Irish spies. When on the
road, Notre Dame preferred not to use the opponent's facilities
before the game. It was bad enough that everybody had tape of
everybody else to study, but to watch the opponent go through
their final preparations was like throwing the game.

Elijah found himself in a hallway. Several of the Baylor players were coming across the lobby in his direction. He turned,
and when he saw the sign for a men's room he darted inside. He
locked himself into a stall and waited, holding his breath. Only
guilt could explain his conviction that the eyes of the world were

upon him. The players came into the room and he lifted his size-sixteen shoes out of sight and waited. Only after they had been gone from the rest room for several minutes did he emerge. When he came outside, the United Limo was not where he had left it.

It was nowhere in sight. It was gone.

Elijah retained powerful memories of a history lecture of the previous year when the professor was speaking of the Battle of Borodino and the fate of Napoleon's march on Moscow. Borodino was not unique, if the professor was right, in having been decided by contingencies that might easily have thrown the fortunes of battle in an opposite direction. The unstated conclusion was drawn that so it is in life. The crucial moment is ambiguous; it can go either way.

Elijah's eyes lifted and he saw across the intersection a large sign atop a motel. $23.95. But it was not the bargain price that drew him. He was lucky with the light and was across the intersection in a minute and pushing through the entrance to the motel. He got out a credit card and asked for a room. After he signed the registration, the clerk wrinkled his nose.

"The card says Phipps. What's this? M-a-r-c . . ."

"That's my middle name." He turned the slip toward him and added *Phipps*.

A key was slid across the counter. "You want to occupy it right away?"

"Yes."

It was not yet nine in the morning. "I've been up all night," Elijah said.

"So have I."

There was an odd antiseptic smell in the corridor and the carpet had a worn track down the middle. When he closed the door behind him and looked at the bed, he knew why he had come. Within a minute he was sound asleep.

160

28

FENWICK HAD ASKED WATTS TO come along to a hush-hush meeting with the woman who was sports information director and a small man Watts did not at first recognize as the coach. The meeting was in the vice president's office, and there were nothing but gloomy faces when they arrived. No wonder. The quarterback was missing and the question was what to do about it.

"I thought he was a mature young man."

"He is, Father. I can't understand this."

The vice president frowned. "What I am about to tell you must go no farther than this room."

Everyone sat forward.

"The police have been here to talk about Phipps."

"They came to me, too," the sports information director said. The coach tried to kick her without being seen by the priest. The vice president himself frowned. "What about?" he asked.

"Oh, it was crazy."

"Tell me."

"They said they found the print of his shoes on the University Club parking lot where that woman was killed."

"What do you say?"

"That they were nuts. One, half the team wears the same make of shoe. Two, size sixteen is not all that unusual with football players. It could have been any of them."

"That's not very helpful," the coach said.

"I meant it was none of them. They all cut through there

after practice. Why should that link them with that poor woman?"

"I am glad you told me this," the vice president said, and he obviously meant it. Watts wondered what he had responded when the police came to him. "We will of course cooperate in every way."

"Where's my quarterback?" the coach asked.

"We have a man hired to track him down, Coach."

"Philip Knight?" It was the first thing Watts had said. Fenwick just nodded or shook his head at what others said.

"How did you know that?" The vice president was angry.

"Logic."

Fenwick kicked him.

"He was hired to represent the university in the Hazel Nootin matter. This is connected with that, or thought to be."

The vice president nodded. "You're right. That is logical. Anyway, Knight will spare no effort, Coach. We want Phipps on the field Saturday."

"I hope nothing has happened to him," Fenwick said, and everybody stared at him. "Of course nothing has," he added.

Outside, Fenwick walked with rigid shoulders rapidly down the hall. "I hate meetings like that," he hissed.

"A meeting of minds," Watts said.

"Oh, shut up."

"It was a good idea, assuring them that nothing had happened to Phipps."

Fenwick stopped and confronted his contemptuous inferior. But they were joined by the sports information director, who tossed her reddish hair and widened her green eyes at Watts. "Good for you."

"I thought he would clobber you for stealing his thunder," Fenwick said.

"You should go to more of these meetings."

And off she went. Fenwick was fuming. All in all, it had been a successful meeting. Watts started to whistle and Fenwick walked faster, trying to get ahead of him, but Watts increased his speed and kept at the side of his alleged superior.

"Maybe I should check this out with Philip Knight."

"Why don't you do that," Fenwick barked. And then he said, "It's only logical."

Victory over such a foe provided only a passing satisfaction. The performance in the vice president's office was the more enjoyable because Fenwick owed his appointment to the priest on the basis that he was married to a shirttail relative of the vice president. It was what people referred to as affirmative nepotism.

Since he was nearby, Watts went to Roger Knight's office, proceeding down the oddly proportioned steps that made it impossible to descend right, left, right, left. One had to put both feet on each slab and then go for the next. It broke the concentration of Watts's thinking, and after coming down the hall to Roger Knight's door, he stood there a moment, hand poised before knocking, gathering his thoughts.

"Come in!"

The Huneker Professor of Catholic Studies had pulled his chair to the window, where he had apparently been looking outside. The screensaver was visible on the monitor of his computer, a Latin sentence: CUM ENIM INFIRMO, TUNC FORTIS SUM. The day when Watts might have deciphered that was long gone. Roger still faced the window.

"Christopher Watts."

The great head nodded. "I saw you by the window." He still had not turned. "When I look out past the cars and trees to the lake I try to imagine what it looked like in eighteen eighty-six, when the remains of Orestes Brownson were brought here."

"Check Schlereth's book. There may be contemporary photographs."

"No. I already have."

He turned slowly, but his eyes were lidded in thought. "Place is as mysterious as time. It doesn't slip away and cease to be. It just stays there under all the layers of time, still the same place no matter what events have gone on there. Taken place. Isn't that a lovely phrase? X took place at Y. To be is to take a place." He grinned suddenly. "Take a seat."

"Elijah Phipps, the quarterback, is missing."

"That's public now?"

"Of course you knew. Your brother has been commissioned to find him."

"Not an easy task."

"It should be hard for a man that size to hide."

"Do you think so? If you wanted to hide a sequoia, where would you put it?"

"In Sequoia National Forest."

"Exactly."

"Where is the Phipps National Forest?"

"Once we know that, we will know where he is."

29 PHIL PARKED HIS CAR IN A
spot on Main Street and walked two blocks
south to the Independent Protestant Church of Jesus Christ and
His Almighty Parent. The address for Edwina Marciniak and the
church were identical. Did she live there? In any case, it seemed
certain that her office would be there.

Downtown South Bend seemed to be emerging from its
bombed-out condition at last. Long ago, urban renewal had lev-
eled it, and for decades its center had consisted of a moonscape
turned into a species of parking lots. Now buildings of the kind
thought modern were rising, fulfilling some of the promises made
by a series of mayors who had presided over the flow of retail
sales to the malls of Mishawaka to the east.

The massive mausoleum of the *Tribune* seemed a monument
to the ending of an era. Did they imagine that what were now
called the print media would play a role in the electronic future?
The New York Times and the other great eastern papers had already made the transition to the Web. A used-car dealer's plastic pennants slapped menacingly in the slight breeze as he
crossed Lasalle.

Edwina Marciniak's church was all but lost among the an-
nexes and addenda to Memorial Hospital. To liken this to the situation of St. Patrick's in Manhattan would have been fanciful,
but the church did seem diminished by all that attention to bod-
ily health. A walkway ran along the side of the church and,
peeking around the corner, Philip saw a flight of stairs and a
door with CHURCH OFFICE conspicuous on it. As he grew closer,

he made out as if it were the next line on an eye chart REV. E. MARCINIAK, PASTOR. In the lower right-hand corner was the invitation *Knock and Enter.* It sounded almost biblical. Philip followed instructions.

As he went down the hallway toward the open door through which he could see a desk, Philip heard grunting sounds and the regular back-and-forth of an exercise machine. This was located in a room just shy of the office. Edwina Marciniak, in jogging costume, sweatband around her head, was hard at work on a NordicTrack. Her eyes were closed, her breath came in great gasps, and perspiration ran down her cheeks. Suddenly she became aware that she was being observed and, flustered, tried to bring the contraption to a halt. In the course of doing this she lost her balance and fell sideways. Philip arrested her fall, righted her, and said hello.

"Wait in my office. I will be with you in a minute."

"I am Philip Knight."

Arms akimbo, she studied him. She shook her head. "No. You can't be."

"Roger Knight is my brother," he told her.

"I find that difficult to believe."

"So do I, much of the time."

"You have the same parents?" Edwina asked blatantly.

Philip was used to surprise at his relationship to Roger, but Edwina Marciniak's attitude veered toward outright skepticism. She decided that there was no need for her to change before settling behind her desk.

"The Notre Dame quarterback is missing," Philip said without preamble.

"Is that right?"

"You don't seem surprised."

Edwina moved objects about on her desk. Her smile grew. "It is now Friday. Tomorrow is the game. If the Notre Dame quarterback is missing, that is, of course, an important development."

"Roger seemed to think you might know more about it."

"More than what?"

"More than we do. My employers think the same."

"Your employers?"

"The university has hired me to look into the disappearance of Phipps. I am a private investigator. A Baptist minister named Stone has gotten in touch with the university. He remembered that you had met Phipps at his church, Hope Baptist."

" 'Met him' is euphemistic. I literally ran into Elijah when I was escaping from the church. It was not an auspicious meeting. He laughed when he was told I am a minister and pastor of this church."

"Stone said that Phipps might be psychologically confused about Saturday's game. Baylor is a Baptist institution. Phipps is a Baptist."

"Far more of a Baptist than Stone."

"In what way?"

"He appreciates the conflict of interest involved in playing against a team that represents a Baptist university. Stone is a rabid Notre Dame fan."

"Where is Phipps now?"

"Do you imagine I know that?"

"Let me put it this way: Notre Dame is prepared to interest the prosecutor in bringing a charge of kidnapping against you unless you cooperate in our effort to locate Phipps."

"That is absurd. You have no reason to think I know anything."

"There you are wrong," Philip told her. "The driver of the United Limo identified a photograph of you. He described how you spirited a passenger onto the bus, making certain that he did not get a good look at him."

"Well, if he didn't get a good look—"

"The clerk in a convenience store where the limo stops in LaPorte says that Elijah came in there to buy candy when the limo stopped there."

"Candy!"

"We know you packed him a lunch. The lunchbox was discovered in the seat Phipps had occupied."

"You seem to have found out everything but where Elijah is."

"Where is he?"

"I do not know. Let me add that even if I did, I would not help you. Have me arrested if you like. I am more than willing to be the victim of injustice in such a cause as this."

"What cause?"

"Insuring the defeat of Notre Dame at the hands of a Baptist football team!" Edwina shouted.

Edwina rose from her chair as she said this and there was fire in her eyes.

"Well, you've told me what I came to find out."

Phil stood. His fingers were still crossed. The M&M's wrapper found in the bus seat had been the basis for the conjecture about Phipps buying candy at LaPorte. The driver had not been positive whether a passenger had gone into the store. But then he was not sure whether Phipps had gone all the way to O'Hare, either. Waring was in contact with Waco on the guess that Elijah had flown home.

The morning *Tribune* had run as headline on page one: WHERE IS ESP?

30

ELIJAH SLEPT FOR HOURS IN his motel room and when he awoke he was hungry. There was a card by his telephone instructing him how he could order a pizza. He immediately did so.

"How long will it take?"

"Half an hour."

"Is there a restaurant in the motel?"

"Naw. All we got is machines," he was told.

Elijah went in stocking feet to a little room just off the lobby. There were coin-operated machines that sold candy and gum and prophylactics. Elijah bought a Baby Ruth and a Mounds bar and went back to his room to wait for his pizza.

He had nodded off again when his phone rang. "Your pizza's here. Should he bring it to the room?"

"Where else?" Elijah said.

"Guests like a warning first."

The pizza arrived in a big red rubberized container to keep it warm. The delivery boy was a girl with short-cut hair and big loopy earrings. He gave her ten dollars, indicating that she could keep the change.

"Thanks a lot. The pizza is thirteen ninety-five."

"This little thing?"

"Hey, you're paying for delivery. I take more than half an hour, you get it for half price."

"I wasn't timing you."

"My boss was."

He gave her another five. She still stood there. He gave her another dollar. He kept two ones, wanting to get some Coke from the machine down the hall. He closed the door after the girl, then waited before opening it again. She was still there, stuffing money into her pockets. She looked startled.

"Where's my receipt?"

The pizza had actually cost $9.95. She was practically crying now that she had been caught. She told him she always overcharged when she delivered pizza to this dump. Half the callers were so drunk they didn't remember ordering.

"Bring me two Cokes and we'll forget it."

She scampered away and came back with the Cokes.

"You'll really forget it?" she pleaded.

"Forget what?" But then he smiled. She punched his arm and hurried away.

It wasn't much of a pizza, more tomato than anything and a thin crust that wasn't crisp the way Elijah liked it. He thought of the dining hall at Notre Dame and how he could be loading up his tray. Still, the pizza took the edge off his hunger. He turned on the television, but a guy was chattering about the games to be played tomorrow. Elijah turned it off. He pulled the blinds and got back into bed.

It was dark when he awoke. He lay for a moment to make sure, and then he was sure. He didn't feel hungry. He swung his legs off the bed and pulled back the drapes of the window. It was dark outside. Thirty yards away was a neon sign advertising the Pagoda Spa. Elijah thought of the hot tubs in Loftus and how great it was to get into one after practice. He wondered if the Pagoda had hot tubs.

He looked them up in the phone book. When he tried to dial it, the voice from the desk came on.

"You want to make an outside call?"

"Do I dial nine first?"

"I'll dial it for you."

Elijah gave him the number.

"What number is that?"

"Do you know anything about the Pagoda Spa?"

"Hey, you can't have them coming over here. You've got to go over there."

"Do they have hot tubs?"

"I guess."

"I just go over there?"

"People do."

Elijah pulled his coat about him, zipped it to the neck, and pulled the hood over his head. It was cool when he stepped outside. He looked up, but the night sky was made invisible by all the artificial lighting. There was a restaurant across the road. He stopped and concentrated and realized that he did not feel hungry at the moment. At the end of the parking lot, he could see the sign of the Pagoda Spa. It seemed to have a parking lot separated from the one that served the motel only by a little band of weeds. The thought of sinking up to his armpits in hot, churning water got his feet going and he headed toward the Pagoda.

There were only a few cars parked out front. As Elijah approached, a man came out of the door of the spa, ducked his head, and hurried to his car. The entrance of the spa was completely ringed with lighting that flashed on and off, and Elijah had to shade his eyes as he approached. He took the handle of the door carefully, lest someone else come hurrying out, and pulled.

He came into a very small room. A pretty little woman in a kimono rose and put her hands together and bowed to him. Elijah, feeling a little foolish, bowed back. There was a very large man standing with folded arms and an expressionless face to one side of the little woman. The woman asked Elijah in purring tones how she could help him.

"Do you have a hot tub?"

"Oh yes."

"That's what I want."

"What kind of credit card do you want to use?"

Elijah unzipped his coat and got out his wallet. The little

lady had taken a credit card machine out of a drawer. She placed his card in it and moved something back and forth across it, printing it on a receipt. She handed him back the card and asked him to sign the receipt.

"How much is that?"

"Why don't we figure that out later?"

"Fair enough."

Again she bowed. She turned and opened a door and indicated that he should precede her. He came into a narrow hall and his guide told him just to keep walking. Through open doors Elijah caught sight of men on tables. He paused at one door. A little woman who might have been the twin of his guide was walking barefoot on the back of a man on a table. Pressure on his elbow urged Elijah on. They came into a large room and there was the hot bath.

"You can undress in here." She pulled back a curtain to reveal a little closet like a cell. Elijah, his nostrils now full of the steamy heat emanating from the tub, got out of his clothes. All of them? Apparently. He looked around the curtain. The little woman was not looking his way. He went rapidly to the tub and was about to hop in when she cried out.

"It's hot!"

"I hope so."

Just then were was a great commotion from the front of the building. Shouts, screams, and then a door burst open and two men came running in, holding wallets out in front of them, exhibiting badges. "Raid!" they cried. "This is a raid!"

Elijah had barely turned, in every sense, when a flash went off. There was a photographer with the police.

31

AUSTIN SCHWARTZ DECLARED
the conference a success and, though it was doubtful that what they had done would alter the course of western civilization, Roger Knight was glad to have it behind him. Now he could give his undivided attention to Saturday's big game with Baylor.

"We're going to have to play without Phipps," Phil said.

"No word?"

"Not even Edwina knows where he might be. That he got on the limo at the campus stop is clear. We know he went at least as far as LaPorte. He might have gone all the way to O'Hare. That seemed sure until an hour ago."

A call to the O'Hare Hilton, an impulsive hunch, had revealed a reservation made in the name of Marciniak. Phil and Waring had hopped on a commuter flight and within an hour were talking to the clerk at the O'Hare Hilton.

"He never checked in."

"You're sure."

"Of course I'm sure. And if he didn't check in he had no key and without a key . . ."

Even as this imperious fellow spoke, departing guests were tossing room keys, actually plastic cards, onto the desk. Waring picked up one of the little envelopes and drew forth the plastic card, one end of which was perforated with a code that opened a door. Which door? A number was written on the envelope.

"What is the turnover here?" Waring asked.

"I beg your pardon?"

Waring made himself understood, and a systematic search of rooms whose occupants had checked out and which had not been reassigned was made. Door after door was opened in the hope that the huge figure of Elijah Samuel Phipps would be found deep in sleep on a king-size bed.

There are hunches and then there are hunches, and this one did not pan out. Having returned to South Bend, Waring went to confront Edwina, hoping to put the fear of God into her for aiding and abetting a kidnapping.

Philip begged to be excused and arrived home in time to enjoy the Hungarian goulash Roger had prepared. Their plan to attend the pep rally was still on.

"What will they say about Elijah?" Phil wondered.

Nothing, as it turned out. ESP was not among the players brought forward for the adulation of the crowd. Little Punky Kunert, the backup quarterback, was introduced, but no one attached any significance to it. Inflammatory speeches were given; inspirational feverinos echoed off the rafters and brought the record crowd in the ACC to its feet. Father Riehle invoked the usual blessing on God's team. The band punctuated the festivities with renditions of the fight song, and when at the end the audience rose to sing "Notre Dame Our Mother," there wasn't a dry eye in the place.

"They got away with it," Phil remarked, referring to the absence of the key man on the Notre Dame squad.

"Maybe he'll show up," said Roger.

"I hope so."

This hope was all too soon realized. Phil flipped on the television to catch the late news, and there, filling the screen, was the face of Elijah Samuel Phipps, a still photo, the athletic department's publicity release of the player. This was followed by blurred footage of a raid on a Michigan City massage parlor, but there was no doubt that the huge man in the buff was no other than the missing Notre Dame quarterback. Within a minute Phil was on the phone to Waring, and twenty minutes later the Knight brothers stopped for Waring and then all three headed up Western Avenue toward Michigan City.

When they arrived at the Michigan City lockup, they found that they had been preceded by Messalina, the sports information director, as well as the quarterback coach.

"Have you talked to him?"

"Right now only lawyers are being let in. Cindy is on her way."

"What's it all about?"

But Waring, with Phil in tow, had headed down a hallway to talk with his counterpart on the Michigan City police. Since no one stopped him, Roger wandered after them. As he left the waiting area, he heard the unmistakable voice of Edwina Marciniak. Roger waited, out of sight, to see what Edwina had come for.

"Are you a lawyer?" she was asked when she demanded to see Elijah.

"I am his spiritual adviser."

This met with silence.

"I am the Reverend Edwina Marciniak, pastor of the Independent Protestant Church of Jesus Christ and His Almighty Parent in South Bend. Mr. Phipps has been coming to me for consultation. I must see him at once. Not to admit me to him would be an unpardonable breach of the wall that separates Church and State."

"Okay."

There were protests from the others, but clearly Edwina had won. Roger continued down the hall after his brother and Waring, who had gone into an office. They were coming out again before he got there, led by a man six and a half feet tall and weighing perhaps 150 pounds. This was Captain Bly of the Michigan City police. He took a step backward when he saw Roger.

"It's all right," Philip said. "He's my brother."

"Well, he's heavy enough." Bly began to cough and choke. He seemed to be laughing.

From behind them in the hallway came the nonstop didactic voice of Edwina Marciniak, conveying to her escort the importance of her visit. When she saw Roger and Philip, she pointed and increased her speed.

"Stop those men. They must not be allowed to see my spiritual charge."

"What the hell?" Bly exploded, glaring at the female officer who was accompanying Edwina. "Get that woman out of here!"

"I am Reverend Edwina Marciniak."

"I don't care if you're the duke of Paducah. Civilians aren't allowed back here. Berger, get her out of here."

Edwina stopped and seemed to become more solid. "You will have to use force."

"This is a pastor from South Bend," Roger explained.

"She has been involved in kidnapping our quarterback," Phil added.

"That is scurrilous slander."

"Get her out of here, Berger," Bly said, his tone lower but more menacing.

The officer tried to get a grip on Edwina's arm but was shrugged away. Bly plucked a whistle from his pocket, put it to his mouth, and blew a piercing, ear-shattering screech. Doors flew open and there was the sound of pandemonium as half the police force converged on this little hallway.

"Pick that woman up and take her out to the waiting room. Tie her down if you have to."

Four large officers took Edwina by the extremities and hustled her off down the hall. Her voice was raised in indignant commentary on this, but soon she was gone and the door shut. Bly returned the whistle to his pocket. "I've had that since I was a rookie. A cop should always have a whistle. Now, let's go see the prisoner."

They were taken to a small room, to which, after a minute or two, Elijah was brought. He looked at his visitors without recognition.

"Can we bring the sports information director in here, Captain Bly?"

The desirability of this was discussed. Elijah followed the discussion with wary interest. Bly came to see the value of Roger's suggestion. Messalina came in and identified herself and recognition gleamed briefly in Elijah's eye.

"I've been arrested."

"He was caught up in a raid on a questionable massage parlor," Bly said, shaking his head at Elijah.

"I went there to try the hot bath!"

Bly coughed and choked.

"I thought they were just nice ladies. Now they tell me it is a . . ."

He couldn't say it. His lip trembled. He would be thinking of what his mother and father would say when they heard of this.

"Has he been booked?" Waring asked.

Bly nodded.

"Could you remand him to my custody?"

"On what basis?" Bly wanted to know.

"He has to play football tomorrow. This is the Notre Dame quarterback."

Bly thought he was being kidded. But then it dawned on him that this particular guest of the city had attracted an awful lot of interested parties. "I'll be darned."

"I can't play against Baylor," Elijah said.

"You'd rather stay in jail?"

"I don't want to stay in jail."

"Then you'll have to play football."

"I can't do that."

"Let me talk to him," Roger said.

Agreement would not have been given to this suggestion if Phil hadn't by nods and whispers and nudges conveyed the thought that this was the thing to do at this juncture. The others withdrew, and Roger and Elijah were alone.

32 ⟶
and clear. The sun rose into a pale blue sky across which the vapor trails of jets wrote an evanescent message. It was Halloween and Saturday, and the suburbs of the nation readied themselves for an evening of tricks or treats, hoping to keep the mendicant custom within the bounds of civility. By and large this meant that the children of one household brought home candy from other households, and vice versa. This equitable distribution of property was encouraged by adults, endured by children, and entered into with gusto by teenagers.

It was also Reformation Day. Four hundred years ago in an obscure German university town, an Augustinian monk went public with his theological difficulties, nailing ninety-five theses to the cathedral door, inviting discussion of them. His name was Martin Luther. Whether or not he was fully aware of it, his deed wrote finis to centuries of a more or less united Christendom. His protest signaled the beginning of the modern world, for good and for ill. In the United States, Christians were divided between Catholics and Protestants, the latter becoming a catch-all term including the most diverse creedal persuasions.

Of less cosmic moment but of supreme importance, in South Bend, Indiana, this was the day of the Baylor–Notre Dame game. The two teams had never before met. There was no tradition, at least as yet. Once, Southern Methodist had been an opponent that added the zest of a religious war to the struggle on the gridiron. Fans on either side had looked on victory or defeat as a sign of divine favor or disfavor. Was the contest to be joined this day the first in a series that would stretch into the unimaginable future?

It was not unfair to say that Baylor had sought this game eagerly. The football program at the Waco school was a strong one. In recent years, they had won victories that had caught, however fleetingly, the eye of the nation. But that eye passed on. There are a few teams that are the perpetual cynosure of the sportswriter's eye, and Notre Dame is one of them. For Baylor to have Notre Dame on its schedule thus insured national attention. The odds were massively against the visitors. Two touchdowns and a field goal, the odds makers had said, would be the margin of victory. There was little money to be made by betting on Notre Dame. Betting on Baylor got one very good odds indeed, but then such a bet was more hopeful than prudent. No matter. A gallantly played loss would be an unequivocal boon to the Baylor program.

This is not to say that the coaches and players had come north to lose. No athlete accepts the inevitability of defeat. In the cant phrase, on any given Saturday any team can beat any other team. And on this Saturday, the Baylor squad was filled with the confidence that they would emerge from the contest victorious, covered with glory, recognized as a national power.

Already at nine o'clock the campus walks were filled with people. Scattered over the grounds were the portable barbecue pits with which one student organization or another would provide food for the crowd and a small profit for itself. Smoke rose from the smoldering charcoal.

Counters were prepared, awnings raised, protective umbrellas opened since the prediction was for a sunny day. In the distance, scarcely audible, came the recorded strains of music from open dormitory windows. In this form the Irish fight song was first heard on this day. Soon the marching band, the oldest in the nation, would gather in front of the main building and put on an impromptu concert before forming up and beginning the march to the stadium. Fans fell in with the band, feet moved with the rhythmic pounding of the drum, excitement mounted.

The enlarged stadium housed eighty thousand fans. The parking lots to the north of the campus were filling up. Many began the long walk past the laundry and maintenance building, past the credit union, along the street lined by the University Press, the Ave Maria Press, and the AeroSpace Building, past Flanner Tower and the library, and then on the final leg to the stadium itself. The band too had now arrived and was playing a final version of the fight song before entering the stadium. By this time, most fans were in their seats, watching the preliminary practices of the two teams.

Baylor players came onto the field determined not to be influenced by the hundred images they had seen of it on television. This was one of the truly legendary football fields in the nation. But they must not be awed; they must not lose heart. They were here to win. And their entrance for practice was greeted by a loyal contingent of fans. If this was the Colosseum and the Irish the lions, the Baptists had supporters in the stands. Nor were they willing to concede that their role today would be that of sacrificial victim.

Eventually the teams left the field, the flag was raised, the national anthem played, the Notre Dame band led by the Baylor band director, and finally "America the Beautiful" was sung. Notre Dame had won the toss and—a mild surprise—elected to receive. The teams took their positions on the field.

For a moment it might have been a still picture. The ball was on its tee; the Baylor kicker, with his teammates lined up on either side of him, waited for the whistle. The Notre Dame special team had a number of stellar players, but none more so than Salvatore Mango. Once he had his hands on the ball, he was a threat to go all the way, no matter the number of opponents he had to thread through.

The whistle blew. The Baylor kicker advanced methodically

on the ball, drawing back his leg, and then brought it forward in a perfect arc; the ball lifted high into the October air, taking with it the delighted cheers of eighty thousand fans, ecstatic that the game was finally under way. The ball had been directed away from Mango. But this prudent caution was soon negated. Hoyle, who had caught the ball, ran on a diagonal toward midfield, and Mango did the same from his side. When they passed, the ball was transferred and Mango was on his way.

He was nearly brought down moments after taking possession of the ball, but the valiant Hoyle threw his body at the foe, upending the would-be tackler, and Mango spurted free. The run would be played in slow motion many times that weekend. It was just what the Notre Dame fan had hoped for and what the Baylor fan had dreaded. The kick had been meant to prevent just this. But Mango had the ball and moved downfield, eluding this pair of clutching hands, leaping high to hurdle over a rolling block that would have knocked the pins out from under him. He reached midfield, he went to the forty, to the thirty, to the twenty-five. Tens of thousands of pairs of eyes could already see him crossing the goal line, so inevitable did it appear. But it was not to be.

Scott Moore, the kicker, had dropped back after sending the ball downfield and now only he stood between the onrushing Mango and the goal line. Would Notre Dame score on the opening kickoff? As if the enormity of that possibility inspired him, Moore made a perfect tackle, his arms embracing the churning knees of Mango, bringing him to the ground, but within the five-yard line.

A great groan of disappointment went up, but its sound suggested that it was only triumph delayed. How could Notre Dame fail to score from within the opponent's five-yard line?

The Baylor defensive team trotted onto the field, and from the opposite side the Notre Dame offense. Only now was it clear that Elijah Samuel Phipps, the legendary ESP, was not at quarterback. Instead the diminutive Punky Kunert was in command of the huddle. When the huddle broke and Kunert took up his position behind the center, it was difficult to feel confidence. His voice was audible when he called the signals—high, nervous, uninspiring. The snap and then a dreadful sight. The ball slipped from Kunert's hands and lay for the taking on the ground just behind the defensive line. Kunert was still moving to the right as he should be, only without the ball. And then bodies fell upon the ball. A mound of uniformed flesh formed over it, and the officials began the task of prying the players from the pile to discover who had possession of the ball. As players stood, they began to gesture. Notre Dame men signaled that the Irish had retained the ball. Baylor men pointed in the opposite direction as they jumped up and down.

The Baylor men were right. The fumble had been recovered by the visitors. For the first time the thought occurred to the most loyal Irish fan: We could lose this game. Until we win this game, until it is over, the opponent can snatch victory from us as they had just taken away the almost certainty of a touchdown.

Foley, the Baylor quarterback, put methodically into execution the game plan the coaching staff had worked out over many months: a combination of short runs, handoffs, laterals, passes over the line, so that in a time-consuming drive the Baylor eleven moved steadily downfield. It was their twelfth play that got them across the midfield stripe. The next play was another run, into the heart of the Notre Dame line. No gain. On the next play, Foley handed off, but no, he still had the ball—he had fooled the Irish defense. He moved to his right and then threw the ball in a great curving arc at a point completely unoccupied when the ball left his fingers. But when it came down, the Baylor receiver streaked under it, caught it on the move, and swept across the Irish goal line. Baylor had scored on their first possession!

------➤

The mood of a game can be set by an early score, particularly when it has come off the opponent's error. There was a palpable uneasiness among Irish fans when little Kunert once more took up his stance behind the center. The ball was snapped, he had it, he wheeled to hand it off, but no one was there. After a split second of hesitation, he began to run. Away from the line, hoping to avoid the Baylor defenseman pursuing him. He was tackled, for an eight-yard loss. An errant pass and a two-yard gain on a running play and the punter jogged onto the field.

His kick was deflected by a Baylor player who rose high in the air with his two arms extended. The ball went out of bounds on the Baylor 49: excellent field position for the visiting team. Philip looked at Roger.

"I thought you talked to Phipps."

"I did."

Phil's look was accusing. After Roger had been left alone with the arrested quarterback in the Michigan City jail, fifteen minutes had gone by. When Roger came out, he had not responded when Phil asked him what he had said to Phipps.

"Is he going to be all right?" Phil had then asked.

"I think so."

"Will he play?"

"He will go back to campus with us."

"Thank God," Phil said.

On the drive home, Philip had told Roger of the nightmares he had been having imagining Kunert filling in for Phipps.

"He was a great high-school quarterback, but he isn't tall enough for this level of play. He can't see over the line, so how can he spot his receivers?"

"Being backup is no small thing."

"He hasn't had fifteen minutes of playing time in three years."

Of course Kunert was a stalwart on practice teams. He had been studying the Baylor films and playing the role of Foley in scrimmages meant to simulate the problems of the game. His grasp of the Notre Dame playbook had grown rusty from lack of playing time and learning the offense of so many different opponents so he could provide a maximum test for the Notre Dame defense as they prepared for a game. If the fans were surprised to see Kunert running the team, Kunert himself seemed the most surprised person in the stadium.

The score at the quarter was Baylor 10, Notre Dame 0.

In the second quarter Baylor made two field goals and Notre Dame one, a historic fifty-two-yard attempt into a light wind. When it hit the crossbar and bounced high above it, the stadium fell totally silent. And then the ball dropped—on the other side of the bar. The relieved cheerings were almost sheepish. Baylor ran out the clock for the remaining twenty seconds. Half-time score: Baylor 16, Notre Dame 3.

NICHOLAS OWENS, FROM HIS place high in the student section, found himself concentrating more on the frantic efforts of Agatha and other members of the cheerleading squad than on the fortunes of the game. The efforts of the cheerleaders increased in inverse ratio to Notre Dame's fortunes, and the shapely agility of Agatha was a consolation in what Nicholas saw as a gloomy prospect.

From the second quarter on, there had emanated from the student section repeated demands for the regular quarterback: "Phipps! Phipps! Phipps!" Over and over again. Others elsewhere in the stadium took it up, and then the cheerleaders themselves chimed in. By halftime the air was filled with an incessant demand that Elijah Samuel Phipps be put into the game.

"He's not on the sidelines," someone to the right of Nicholas said.

"I heard he got caught in a raid."

"At Bridget McGuire's?"

"He's got to be of age."

"Michigan City."

"Michigan City! What's in Michigan City?"

A cheerleader was being passed up the student body, held high above their heads. She was being lifted from one level to the next. On the sidelines her fellows cheered on the effort. When the cheerleader got to him, Nicholas realized it was Agatha.

For a brief moment her face was inches from his own. Her face was flushed with exertion and excitement. Her breath was sweet on his face. Involuntarily he leaned forward, but before his lips could meet hers, a roar of protest went up and she was lifted onto the next level above.

"Nice try," Nicholas was told. He shrugged, a blasé man of the world, but he turned and ruefully watched Agatha's progress toward the top row. Once there, she would be released and run down the steps to general cheering. When she was on her feet and bouncing down, her eyes sparkling, her cheeks rosy with health, Nicholas fell in behind her and followed her down. To his dismay, others fell in behind him and by the time he reached field level, Agatha was lost in a crowd of admirers. She was lifted onto the field, and when she turned to express her thanks her eyes met Nicholas's. She seemed to lean toward him over the intervening distance and then her lips puckered into a long-distance kiss.

Of such moments is history made. Nicholas floated back to his seat. Time went on, of course. The cheerleaders did what cheerleaders do during halftime. Everywhere but in the student section there was a steady traffic up and down as fans went for food or comfort. And on the scoreboard, undeniable, unbelievable, stood the score: Baylor 16, Notre Dame 3.

Fig Nootin sat huddled in his seat, feeling guilty to be attending a game so soon after Hazel's death. He had held these two seats since his first marriage and kept them after he married Hazel even though she had little interest in football. At most she'd attended one game; for the rest, Fig took as his guest one friend or another. Today his son Alfred sat beside him. Bernie had rejoined his ship in the Mediterranean.

"I'm in no rush to go back," Alfred had said.

He had been home only hours after the tragedy. "I was in the country already."

"How did you hear?"

"Dad, it's on the news."

Thank God for Alfred's support. His son had insisted he attend the game.

"If you stayed home, you'd watch it on TV, right?"

"That's different."

"Sure. You wouldn't be surrounded by eighty thousand strangers."

Alfred was less sure Fig should get back to work right away. Fig told his son he had to finish Roger Knight's bookcases. Alfred went with him when he went around to the Knights'. Roger was home, and that was a treat. Alfred had never met him and Fig doubted his son would believe him if he described the man. The two got along. Fig had left Alfred with Roger and taken the measurements he had come for. When he had worked here before, he had talked of his sons to Roger, maybe too much, but the huge man seemed genuinely interested. And he seemed really interested in Alfred now. So Fig dallied, giving his son more time with the professor.

"How about that guy?"

"His Spanish is pretty good."

"Spanish!"

"Chatters away like a native."

It was one of the things Fig had bragged about, Alfred working in Miami, swimming in the sea of the people, champion of the underclass. Of course you had to know Spanish to do that.

"I wish I'd heard you two going at it."

In the presidential box, Father Molloy was considering his reply after his Baylor counterpart said that he appreciated Notre Dame holding back their best players for the game. Roger Knight came to the rescue, if that was the word for it.

"You mean Phipps, Dr. Sloan? He spent the night in jail."

Sloan laughed at the pleasantry. A Notre Dame vice president scowled at Roger. Dave Solomon drew the attention of the party to the halftime show and his wife, Lou, at least followed his bidding. The Baylor band was executing intricate maneuvers to the tune of "Dixie" and all the transplanted southerners in the stands erupted with delight.

"My daughter wanted so much to do graduate work at Notre Dame, Father Malloy. In medieval studies."

"We must look into that."

Dave Solomon piped up. "Dr. Sloan has eight children."

"My daughter applied," Sloan said.

"Make a note of that, Pickle."

It was an awkward moment. Roger engaged President Sloan in conversation then, beginning with medieval studies and going on to other things. Then he said, "But tell me about Foley."

"Foley?"

"Your quarterback."

On the field the Baylor band gave way to the Notre Dame band. The drum major pranced onto the field, his head thrown so far back as to be parallel with the ground he trod upon. It is a minor skill, but not everyone can walk while bent over backward under the eyes of eighty thousand fans without mishap. Arrived at his destination, he straightened, spun, and began to flail his arms in rhythmic direction.

In the box, Roger nodded through President Sloan's response to his question and then fell silent. Some minutes later he rose to his feet, accepting the offers of help as he did so. He smiled apologetically and then went beneath the stands.

The halftime clock ticked down and the Baylor team returned to great applause from the eastern side of the field. Notre Dame fans looked toward the tunnel from which their heroes would emerge. The seconds ticked by. Was some great surprise in store? Once Dan Devine had sent his squad out clad not in the traditional gold and blue, but in green. The stadium had gone wild. The gimmick had been effective, but it had never been repeated. Those green uniforms were now a collectors' item.

A single figure appeared at the opening of the tunnel. A girl, a trainer, her flowing hair emerging from the opening at the back of her cap. She looked back the way she had come, and still the Irish did not appear. Then, in a burst, they came out of the tunnel and onto the field, led by the cheerleaders, one of whom held high before him a massive banner with ND on it. He might have been a Marine about to plant the Stars and Stripes on Iwo Jima. And then the chant of the first half began again, but with a very different timbre.

"Phipps, Phipps, Phipps!"

And there, suited up, running onto the field beside the coach, was the unmistakable figure of Elijah Samuel Phipps. The field announcer was saying something but he was drowned out. The fans already knew that this half would not be like the previous one. Now Notre Dame would be led by its Heisman Trophy candidate. Punky Kunert could sit on the sidelines, grateful that he had not gotten Notre Dame into any deeper hole than he had. The game plan could now be put into execution.

But Baylor was to receive, and it was the Notre Dame kicking team that took the field. There was a sustained cheer as the kicker set himself, waited for the whistle, and then, letting his arm drop, started toward the teed-up ball. The cheer rose in volume and then toe met pigskin. Eyes rose to follow the presumed trajectory, but the ball could not be seen. It had not lifted but had gone screaming toward the oncoming Baylor team about ten feet off the ground. As it descended it struck a lineman's helmet and veered to the left. Here it went as if predestined into the hands of the safety who had sixty-five yards of Irishless turf between him and the goal line. Hysterical mothers lift vehicles off their children, swimmers hold their breath under water beyond human endurance, and athletes encumbered with heavy equipment run like gazelles in similar circumstances. And the Baylor ball carrier streaked down the field with desperate Irish defenders vectoring after him for half the run, but there was no way in the world he could be prevented from crossing the goal line. The vast majority in the stadium sat in stunned silence as the Baylor team celebrated. They lined up quickly for the point after, and the kicker sent it solidly between the uprights. Baylor 23, Notre Dame 3. Could even Elijah Samuel Phipps overcome such a deficit against a scrappy and now inspired opponent?

The answer was yes. Phipps passed for one touchdown and ran for another before the third quarter was half over, and with 23–17 on the scoreboard, the mood among the Irish fans changed. Phipps played with authority, directing his team with the touch of a master. But Baylor rallied after the second touchdown and dug in, refusing to give ground. Three times in a row it was three downs and punt on Irish possessions. Going into the fourth quarter, all fans watched with rapt attention, collectively aware that they were witnessing a historic game. At the beginning of the fourth quarter, on first down, Baylor threw a pass of the kind that teams throw in desperation in the closing seconds of a game. Caught unprepared, the Irish defense once more lost a race into their own end zone. That quickly, the score was 29–17. The extra point brought the score to 30–17.

When Notre Dame got the ball, they used the mirror of the Baylor play on first down with identical results. After the successful extra point it was 30–24. There is that in the Notre Dame fan which makes him intolerable to others, namely, his unassailable confidence that in a well-ordered universe Notre Dame is meant to win all of its games. If from time to time a loss occurs, this can be ascribed to bad officiating, unsportsmanlike conduct on the part of the opponents, or simply an act of God in the form of torrential rain or debilitating sleet. This is the attitude of fans, not of players, the latter being far more sensitive to the vagaries of fortune. But at this point of the game, the Notre Dame team shared a common conviction. With Phipps at the controls, the game was theirs to be won. But no fruit was borne of this confidence, and when Baylor had the ball they used the full allotment of time for each play, and sometimes more, but they willingly took the penalty in order to prolong the agonized impatience of the fans in the stadium. On third down, Baylor tried to draw the Irish off sides, but discipline held, the clock ran out, and it was fourth down with fifteen yards to go. The Baylor punter took the snap, but as he rotated the ball to get the seams where he wanted them, it slipped loose, bounced once, and was covered by a Baylor player. No matter. The ball went over to the Irish on their own forty-five-yard line.

There was a minute showing on the clock when the Irish lined up. The snap came and, as the play developed, it seemed a repetition of the Hail Mary that had served them so well in the previous quarter. The Baylor defense dropped back and almost to a man took off after the wide end, who was loping down the sidelines. Phipps stood four yards beyond the line of scrimmage.

"He doesn't have the ball!"

"Where's the ball?"

And then attention turned to the opposite side of the field and the Notre Dame back who, having taken a handoff from Phipps that no one had seen, was all but strolling across the goal line: 30–30. There was less than a half-minute on the clock. Notre Dame took a time-out—its last. The situation was clear to all, friend and foe alike. If Notre Dame successfully kicked the extra point, they would be in the lead by one point and Baylor would not have enough time to counter. The teams formed and then a whistle blew. Baylor had called a time-out. Once more the teams trotted to the sidelines. The tension in the stands was at an all-time pitch. Once more the teams lined up. Eighty thousand fans held their breath. Another whistle! Baylor had called time-out again, using its full quota. There was a groan from the stands and the Irish players too seemed edgy as they left the field. As a psychological ploy it was inspired. All the principals had had time to reflect on what they must do. The center must snap the ball. The holder must get it set up properly. The kicker must put the ball between the uprights. The offensive line had to protect the kicker so he could do his task. The task before the defenders was equally plain, but delay served rather to concentrate the mind than to induce nervousness.

For the final time the teams lined up. No whistle now could

delay the outcome. The official indicated that play should begin. The snap was perfect, the setup perfect. The kicker executed the set number of steps as he advanced and brought the side of his foot into the ball. It lifted, just cleared the clawing fingers of a defender, and hooked toward its destination—hooked more than the kicker had intended. Much more. A gasp went up when the ball hit the left upright. It seemed to be suspended in air, then hovered like the Goodyear blimp above the stadium. And then it fell. The officials gave no immediate indication, but then the signal came.

The ball had not gone over the crossbar. The score stood at 30–30.

The game ended in a tie in regulation.

Not everyone in the stadium was certain of what must happen next. If this had been the previous year, overtime would have been mandatory, a sudden-death decision. But during the winter meetings of the NCAA that rule had been changed. 30–30 was the final score.

Father Malloy shook President Sloan's hand. The Baylor president was in a state of semishock.

"Is it over?"

"That's it. Great game."

"We didn't lose?"

"Far from it," Roger said. "You have won a great moral victory."

34 ROGER AND PHILIP HAD BEEN invited to a postgame party at the Morris Inn, and Solomon insisted that they come.

"I want to hear all about the conference," he said in his scratchy voice.

But in the manner of postgame parties, it was the game that was the topic of conversation. High administrative officers expressed their satisfaction with the outcome of the game. President Sloan said that he hoped to welcome all those present in Waco when the teams met again.

"Where's Waco?" someone asked.

Pickle circulated, smiling relentlessly, clutching a glass of mineral water. He and Roger toasted one another's abstemiousness.

"I had never thought of water when someone asked: Animal, vegetable, or mineral?"

Pickle tittered.

Ronald Arbuthnot stood at Roger's elbow and said, "I must say again how much I enjoyed your paper."

"Choosing the topic was not easy. I had thought of discussing Brownson's defense of the papacy."

Arbuthnot turned his head and looked at Roger out of the corner of his eye. "Naughty, naughty."

"I am a convert myself."

"What were you before?" Arbuthnot asked.

"Lukewarm."

"I am saved, of course."

"I aspire to the same condition."

"Ho ho."

In the University Club, Debbie seemed the one cool head in a crowd of drunks. Her blond hair was swept back from her noble brow; her skeptical eye monitored the scene before her.

"Happy Reformation Day," a man said, reeling past her.

"It's about time."

One fan in the back bar was diagramming a play on a paper napkin that was soggy with scotch and seemed indifferent to his *X*'s and *O*'s. "We could have won that game!" he cried to Earl.

"We should have won that game," the bartender agreed.

Waitresses moved with trays throughout the crowd, avoiding elbows and gesticulating hands, renewing the libations of the celebrants.

Agatha had waited on the field after the game, as if she expected Nicholas to join her. Trying to get to her through the intervening mass of bodies had the aspect of a nightmare, but their eyes had met and, without benefit of wire or sound, an agreement reached. Finally, bedraggled and breathless, he reached her side. They stood looking at one another, neither knowing what to say.

"Some game."

"A tie!"

"Still."

"You're right. We could have lost."

"To Baylor."

His hand had found hers. He held it tentatively and then she gripped his tightly and the kiss they had not had when she had been handed up the stands was consummated. Then, still holding his hand, she ran with him off the field. No triumphant athlete had felt more elation than Nicholas Owens as he exited the field with Agatha Marciniak.

SPORTSWRITERS AND FANS

waited docilely in the press room beneath the stadium for coaches and players to appear. Edwina bowled through the gathering and on into the locker room. Cries of protest went up, but she waved her hand and cried, "Clergy!" and the protests subsided. Edwina felt that she was beneath the Colosseum in Rome, on her way to upbraid a Christian who had capitulated at the sight of the lions. She found a towel-draped Elijah standing by his locker. The look of satisfaction on his face enraged her.

"You have betrayed your ideals."

"No I haven't."

"You have played against a Baptist team."

"I played against Baylor."

"Are you making some subtle point?"

"It was a tie. Nobody won."

"Through no fault of yours. If I believed in witchcraft I would claim credit for that ball not going over the crossbar. I willed it not to go over. I ordered it not to go over. And it did not."

"They deserved a tie."

"Are you saying you threw the game?" Edwina said.

"No! I threw two touchdown passes and we ran for another score. . . ." At the moment the second half was blurred. "I tried to win. We all did."

"I am not talking about the others. You tried to defeat the greatest Baptist university in the land. A Protestant school!"

"You don't understand."

Edwina threw up her arms in angry impatience. "But what can I expect of a man who at such a crucial time went off to the fleshpots of Michigan City?"

"All I wanted was a hot bath."

"And all David wanted was a peek at Bathsheba. You should be ashamed of yourself."

"I don't want my parents to know," he told her.

"Aha!"

"What's that supposed to mean?"

"Is that how they persuaded you to betray your ideals and play that game? Did they threaten to expose your antics in Michigan City?"

"There were no antics!" Elijah insisted.

"Your parents may hear about it in any case."

"Are you going to tell them?" His expression was eloquent: *et tu, Edwina?*

She gave him a long look. "I will not spread scandal. Your sordid secret is safe with me."

"I don't have any secrets. That isn't why I played."

"Why then?"

"Do you know that fat professor, Roger Knight?"

"Indeed I do. What fallacies did he employ to get you to play?"

"No fallacies."

"Then how did he get you to change your mind?"

"Foley."

"Foley! Who is Foley?"

"The Baylor quarterback." Phipps smiled as if for the first time he appreciated the humor of it. "He's a Catholic."

Edwina fell back. She looked at him. Her expression told him that she wanted to believe he was lying, that this was a trick to quiet her accusation. She had obviously relished the role of prophet, had enjoyed haranguing him and telling him the evil he had done. But she would never know the feeling he had when the police burst into the Pagoda Spa shouting that this was a raid. He was standing there in the buff, naked to his enemies, and when they took him away he grabbed a towel and covered himself with that, Adam being thrown out of Eden.

"Let me put on my clothes," he had pleaded with the police.

"You should have thought of that earlier," they'd said.

Everyone had been smirking. This was all a joke of some kind, raiding the massage parlor and rousting out a few stupid men who had wandered in out of who knew what loneliness. They had been hooted at and laughed at, as if there was something comic about wanting a little Oriental lady to walk barefoot over your back and do whatever else, but it wasn't funny. It was sad, sad about the men, and sad about those little ladies, too.

Downtown, when they stopped smirking, they had told him those girls were like slaves and then Elijah had really felt bad, he a black man, the descendant of slaves but raised as a God-fearing Christian, exploiting those poor Oriental women. Even to himself his excuse sounded hollow now: "All I wanted was a hot tub." That was true. He hadn't known what kind of place the Pagoda was, but nobody would believe that. The police hadn't believed it, the sports information director hadn't believed it, just nodded as if that was his story and he should stick to it. Everybody had talked damage control. Everybody but Roger Knight.

"It could have happened to anyone," Roger had said.

"All I wanted was a hot tub."

"How could you know it wasn't what it pretended to be?"

"I wasn't in there five minutes before they raided it."

"You can get a hot tub back on campus."

"I've been running away," Elijah had finally confessed.

Roger Knight was kind of a comic character, too fat, clumsy, looking like he might need help getting from one side of the room to the other, but he really listened when Elijah talked, so Elijah had kept on talking. He told him of his crisis of conscience, of consulting with Pastor Stone, who wasn't any help at all, how he had met Edwina Marciniak there at Hope Baptist, and she saw the seriousness of his problem. She helped him see what he must do.

"Run away?"

"Not play the game. If I stayed around, they would talk me into it. I had to leave."

"Why did you get off at Michigan City?"

He told Knight of the Baylor players and of hiding in the stall in the john and how when he came out the bus was gone. He agreed to go back to campus when Knight assured him that no one could make him play on Saturday. But he shouldn't run away.

It had been right to come back. The coaches and his teammates had tried to take it in stride, but it was pretty obvious what they thought of him. He had stayed in the locker room when they went out the tunnel for the first half and followed the game on television. Studying the Baylor defense, he was certain he could have executed the game plan against them. If he could only forget that they were Baptists, too.

That had all changed when Professor Knight came down at halftime to tell him of the interesting conversation he had just had with the president of Baylor.

"He said they had all remarked how odd it was. The Notre Dame quarterback is Baptist, and their quarterback is Catholic."

"He is?"

"His name's Foley. He played his high-school ball at Fort Worth Catholic."

"A Catholic is directing the Baylor offense?"

"That's right."

He had waited for Elijah to come to the conclusion himself. How could it be wrong to play against a Baptist team that was led by a Catholic? There was cheering in the locker room when Elijah suited up. They were late going onto the field for the second half, but the stadium exploded when he ran to the Irish bench flanked by two coaches while the students chanted his name.

When he told her this after the game in the locker room, Edwina Marciniak just shook her head. She had endured much. She had fought the good fight, and lost. She had run the race, and failed to win. But the unkindest cut of all was to be told that Baylor had a Catholic playing quarterback. Was there no one else in the world who still took religion seriously anymore besides herself?

"It's only a game," Elijah said, to console her. "And Notre Dame didn't win. We tied."

36 ON MONDAY AFTER THE BIG
game, a cold and blustery wind blew fallen
leaves across the campus. Saturday's game was forgotten now,
except by the sportswriters on *The Observer*, who honed their
skills by analyzing how Notre Dame could have won the game,
and should have won the game. Even without Elijah Samuel
Phipps. But the fact of the matter was they hadn't been able to
win the game *with* Phipps.

In the publicity office, a familiar acedia was felt.

"Give it a little time," Fenwick said, "and they'll forget
Hazel Nootin too."

"The police won't," Watts said.

"Then the murderer is safe. When is the last time anyone
was prosecuted for murder in this county?"

"It happens all the time."

"I meant convicted."

Fenwick might be right. Not that Watts would give him the
satisfaction of saying so. It did not seem right that a human
being could be jumped and strangled and left like garbage on
the lawn and the murderer never be caught. How many people
walking the streets had murdered another person—with im-
punity? It was a frightening thought. It was an even more frightening thought that they had suspected him of doing that to
Hazel. Torture, maybe, the infliction of endless pain, but why
would he kill her?

"The university hired a man to find out who killed her," he
told Fenwick.

"Ha."

Fenwick went back to *The Observer*, frowning over the daily crossword. He spent much of the day trying to solve it, usually without success. After a while he would surreptitiously consult a dictionary, but it didn't help. Roger Knight did that puzzle with a ballpoint, allowing himself five minutes and following different patterns—starting now in the lower right corner and working diagonally to the upper left, or beginning in the middle and working first downward and later up. Of late he had been downloading the daily puzzle from *The London Telegraph*, a far greater challenge. Fenwick would have been out of his depth with a kiddie puzzle. Still, it passed away the empty hours in the office of public information.

Watts, trying to keep on the edge of his mind the bottomless thirst that would drive him back to drink in a minute if he let down his guard, picked up his phone and telephoned Waring of the South Bend police to ask about the status of the investigation into the death of Hazel Nootin.

"We don't want any surprise announcements," Watts explained.

"We're checking your alibi again."

"Funny."

"It's not much of a defense, saying you don't know where you were."

"If I was somewhere, I would have been seen."

"Just my point. What are your favorite bars?"

"Waring, if the investigation has degenerated into this, the university has nothing to fear from bad publicity."

He called Philip Knight next. The private investigator said he knew nothing that Waring did not.

"That's not much," Watts commented.

"Do you have any suggestions?" Philip asked.

"What do you mean?"

"What I said."

Watts brought the conversation to a close. He pushed back from his desk, keeping his eye from the bottom left-hand drawer, where solace of a sort was available. He would not give in. It was mind over matter. He decided to stop in on Roger Knight.

He was surprised when he got there to find the office full of people. There was Fig Nootin and one of his sons, as well as two students, a boy and a girl, holding hands. They looked familiar, and no wonder. Nicholas Owens, who had organized the speech at the Knights of Columbus Hall, and Agatha Marciniak, who was the niece of the scourge of Catholicism. Fig was measuring a wall with an eye to installing a bookcase.

"The university will do that for you," Watts said. "You don't have to bring in a contractor."

"Fig will be doing it with a university contract."

"Ah."

Alfred Nootin stood sullenly in a corner, obviously not glad to be there. But then Owens and Agatha left and Roger persuaded Alfred to take a chair. He exclaimed when Alfred crossed his legs.

"That's a pretty large foot."

At the wall, Fig groaned. "Those boys kept me in the poorhouse, growing out of clothes."

"What size are they?"

Alfred shrugged. Watts guessed twelve, thirteen.

"Sixteen," Fig said. "Unless he's shrunk. You sure you want just shelves? I could make you something really beautiful as well as practical. The lower half storage, the upper half bookshelves."

"Bookshelves from top to bottom," Roger said.

"You're the boss."

"Let's go for a walk," Roger said to Alfred, heaving himself to his feet. The young man seemed glad for a chance to leave.

------>

Roger and Alfred crossed the parking lot and went on to a bench on the edge of the path that circled St. Mary's Lake. Far out on the lake, two white swans progressed slowly over the water, followed by a chevron of mallards. In the shallow water along the shore, dozens of Canadian geese moved around importantly. They were on the lawn around the bench as well.

"Their god is their belly," Roger said.

Alfred stared out over the lake.

"They spend every waking moment feeding themselves."

"I wonder what they would taste like?" Alfred said.

"That may be the only solution. They are taking over the country."

But Roger did not sound worried by this prospect. He wasn't sure that he believed it. It was not to discuss the Canadian geese problem that he had asked Alfred to come with him for a walk. Fig had urged his son to go.

"How long do you plan to stay home?" Roger asked Alfred.

A shrug. "Dad seems to be doing all right."

"It will be lonely for him."

Another shrug.

"I suppose that's why he married Hazel: loneliness."

A longer silence. "Maybe."

"What was she like?"

"Not at all like my mother."

"How old were you when your mother died?"

"Twelve," Alfred answered.

"I was younger when both my parents died. Phil raised me."

"He never married?"

"No." A squawk went up and a goose lifted into the air, its legs dangling before they were tucked up and nestled in its underfeathers. One after another, more geese rose. There was no seeming reason for this migration. But soon the commotion ceased. Most geese remained where they had been. "I suppose you wish your father hadn't married."

Alfred turned to look at him, but Roger continued to look out over the lake.

"Your father told me that one day he came home to find that she had gotten rid of all your mother's things."

"To Good Will."

"Do you remember that?"

"Of course."

"Killing her was no solution, Alfred. You have created a much greater problem for yourself—and for your father."

They sat there in such silence as the natural world affords. Everything depended on what Alfred said now. For a long time he said nothing.

"I didn't mean to kill her."

"Strangling someone has that effect."

"That isn't what I was doing. I grabbed hold—"

Roger turned and looked into Alfred's anguished eyes. His expression changed.

"I will deny I said that."

"Did you think I was going to turn you in?"

"Aren't you?"

"No. You are. Alfred, the evidence is all there. They haven't fully realized that yet, but they will. They will know you were in town; Watts will realize that you answered the phone when he called from the club to tell your mother Fig was in the bar; they will identify your prints in the parking lot and in the area around where the body was found. Elijah may identify you."

"Elijah! The quarterback?"

"He cut through the club grounds after the last practice he took before running off. He saw you head across the parking lot with a woman. He thought you were another player. You're big enough."

"What did he do?"

"Went another way."

Tears are signs of many things. Of sorrow, of remorse, of

sadness, of relief. Alfred sat on the bench beside Roger, weeping helplessly. Roger patted his arm. Alfred was a young man now, but it had been a small boy, resentful of the woman who had usurped his mother's role, who had followed her to the club after Watt's call and heard her berate his father in the bar and then followed her out and silenced her as he had wanted to do for so many years. He wept too because he must realize now that nothing was solved by what he had done.

"I came home as a surprise. Dad didn't know I was at the house. But I answered the phone. . . ."

He sat there thinking of all the things that might not have happened and of the one awful deed that he had done.

Fifteen minutes later, they rose from the bench. Alfred helped the overweight professor to the road and then across the parking lot to his office. Fig Nootin's pickup was no longer parked outside.

"Come in," Roger said. "You can use my phone."

Alfred hesitated, but he came with Roger to make the phone call that would begin the long process to restore the delicate balance he had upset.

SOME WEEKS LATER, THE
Knight brothers were dining with Father
Carmody at Holy Cross House. Time had passed since the Baylor game, but not enough so that the result failed to grate on the
nerves of the residents of Holy Cross House. The only blot on the
otherwise unblemished escutcheon of Ara Parseghian was that he
had settled for a 10–10 against Michigan State rather than take
a chance for victory and lose standing in the polls if Notre Dame
failed. The tie with Baylor had not been due to failed effort, but
it was with a team less highly ranked than that with which Ara
had had to contend. There were some who, as years intervened,
professed to understand and even approve the decision that
Parseghian had made in the stress and pressure of the waning
minutes of a game, but Father Carmody was not among them.

"They should not have held back Phipps until the second
half," the father stated.

"He was not available before," Roger assured him.

"Nonsense. It was unpardonable hubris. An attempt to beat
Baylor with a substitute." He paused and apparently against his
will pronounced the name: "Kunert."

"What did you think of Foley, Father?" Phil asked.

"Foley?"

"The Baylor quarterback."

"Lucky."

"The luck of the Irish, then. He is a good Catholic boy."

"The Baylor quarterback?"

"And Phipps, as you know, is a Baptist," Roger said.

Carmody was astounded by what he was being told. "Phipps is a Baptist? That can't be."

"I'm afraid it is."

"The Baptist had a Catholic quarterback and we had a Baptist quarterback?"

"That's right."

Father Carmody digested this incredible information. His mind was obviously reeling. Then he began to nod slowly.

"I understand it all now."

"How so, Father Carmody?" Phil asked.

The priest looked at Roger and Philip, his eyes brimming with a wisdom acquired over many years and after many football seasons.

"God is not mocked, gentlemen. God is not mocked."

—Feast of St. Agatha, 1998